Unfathomed

Anna Hackett

Unfathomed

Published by Anna Hackett
Copyright 2016 by Anna Hackett
Cover by Melody Simmons of eBookindiecovers
Edits by Tanya Saari

ISBN (eBook): 978-1-925539-12-7
ISBN (paperback):978-1-925539-13-4

What readers are saying about Anna's Romances

At Star's End — One of Library Journal's Best E-Original Romances for 2014

Return to Dark Earth — One of Library Journal's Best E-Original Books for 2015 and two-time SFR Galaxy Awards winner

The Phoenix Adventures — SFR Galaxy Award Winner for Most Fun New Series and "Why Isn't This a Movie?" Series

Beneath a Trojan Moon — SFR Galaxy Award Winner and RWAus Ella Award Winner

Hell Squad — Amazon Bestselling Science Fiction Romance Series and SFR Galaxy Award for best Post-Apocalypse for Readers who don't like Post-Apocalypse

The Anomaly Series — #1 Amazon Action Adventure Romance Bestseller

"Like Indiana Jones meets Star Wars. A treasure hunt with a steamy romance." – SFF Dragon, review of *Among Galactic Ruins*

"Strap in, enjoy the heat of romance and the daring of this group of space travellers!" – Di, Top 500 Amazon Reviewer, review of *At Star's End*

"High action and adventure surrounding an impossible treasure hunt kept me reading until late in the night." – Jen, That's What I'm Talking About, review of *Beyond Galaxy's Edge*

"Action, danger, aliens, romance – yup, it's another great book from Anna Hackett!" – Book Gannet Reviews, review of *Hell Squad: Marcus*

Don't miss out! For updates about new releases, action romance info, free books, and other fun stuff, sign up for my VIP mailing list and get your *free box set* containing three action-packed romances.

Visit here to get started:
www.annahackettbooks.com

Chapter One

She hated wearing heels.

Morgan Kincaid scowled down at the offending shoes. She was also wearing a tight, little cocktail dress in a brilliant aquamarine. Eye-catching and bold. Exactly as she'd planned. In addition, she wore far more makeup than usual—which she also hated—but she'd accented her eyes with smoky black and painted her lips red.

She didn't mind the dress that much, except that there was nowhere to store her SIG Sauer. She wrinkled her nose. She hated leaving her handgun behind.

As her heels clicked on the path leading up to the museum entrance, she was glad that she'd at least been able to strap the smallest knife from her collection to her thigh. Not that she should need a weapon for this job.

Morgan looked up and studied the western façade of the Denver Museum of Nature and Science. She liked the eye-catching wall of glass. The modern feel contrasted with the amazing exhibitions on display inside. The museum contained everything from history exhibits, to dinosaur fossils, and even a planetarium.

She paused and turned back to see the view. The museum was perched on the edge of City Park, with a view of the city skyline, and the even more impressive outline of the Rocky Mountains beyond. The entire scene was backlit by the setting sun.

"Morgan, I'm entering the party."

The deep male voice of Declan Ward echoed through the tiny earpiece in her left ear. Dec was her boss at Treasure Hunter Security. After a career in the Navy, Morgan had left when they'd refused to let her join the SEAL teams. After a few months adrift, uncertain what to do with her life, she'd answered a knock on her door to find Dec on her doorstep.

The former Navy SEAL and his brother, Callum, had offered her a job she couldn't refuse. Along with their tech-savvy sister Darcy, the Ward siblings had created a security business to provide protection to archeological digs, expeditions, and high-profile or valuable museum exhibits across the globe.

Morgan liked living in Denver, and she loved working at THS.

She discreetly touched her ear, fiddling with her sparkly, dangling earring. "I'm not far behind you."

"Remember, we've been hired to test the exhibit security of the Mughal Emerald Pendant. Get close to the emerald and check the security. You know what to do."

She certainly did. "You got it."

"And keep an eye out for Coop," Dec added. "He's on the inside."

Morgan fought back a snort. You only saw Ronin Cooper if he wanted you to see him. Also a former SEAL and a former CIA agent, the man was an expert at hiding—in the shadows or plain sight.

She smoothed a hand over her short, black hair. She kept it cut short so it stayed out of her way on missions. She continued on toward the doorway, and the short line of people waiting to enter. As she reached the guard at the doorway, she smiled, upping the charm. She watched interest flicker in the man's eyes, and his gaze dropped down, lingering on her legs. *Men.* They were so predictable.

Out of her small clutch, she pulled her glossy invite for the evening's special exhibit. He checked it, eyed her legs again, and then waved her through.

Morgan stepped into the heart of the party. The western side of the museum had several levels that could be hired for private functions. This level was filled with people dressed to impress, wandering through multiple displays that had been set up. Each one showcased the museum's latest acquisitions.

A collection of priceless jewels of the Mughal Rulers of India.

She checked her coat and then wandered through the crowd. The sounds of quiet conversation, low laughter, and clinking champagne flutes mingled in her ears. Outside, the sun had finally set, and the city spread out below them in a twinkle of lights.

Morgan circled the room, noting all the exits, the stairs leading up to the next level, and the doorways into the kitchen and to the main part of the museum. It was second nature to her. She'd worked in Naval Intelligence prior to passing all the physical tests to join the SEAL teams. She'd wanted to join special forces so much, and follow in her father's footsteps.

The thought of her dad was like a sharp slash of a knife. God, a day never went past where she didn't miss the old guy. Because she had the wrong equipment between her legs, her dreams of special forces had been crushed. Mack Kincaid would have protested loud and proud for his daughter.

Morgan fought back the old bitterness and kept her shoulders relaxed. She was doing good work now, and she loved it. She hoped her dad would be proud.

She did another circle of the party, this time paying attention to the artifacts on display. The jewels were incredible. There was a huge sapphire inlaid with gold and other small gemstones. A small box made entirely of carved emeralds. A large, heart-shaped, diamond pendant.

God, Declan's fiancée Layne would go nuts for this stuff. The archeologist was passionate about her work. Morgan liked history as well, and truly believed it deserved to be protected. But at the end of the day, some of the stuff THS helped uncover and safeguard was just old and ugly.

She turned her head and caught sight of Dec. She was careful not to let her gaze linger on him.

Although, dressed in a sharp suit, the man deserved a second look. She was used to seeing him in cargo pants and T-shirts. In a suit, the man looked mighty fine. Layne would go nuts for that, too. The two of them couldn't keep their hands off each other.

Morgan sighed. She'd seen Declan wet, muddy, sweaty, and—once or twice—naked. While she could appreciate his rugged looks, she wasn't attracted to him. He was like a brother to her. All of her colleagues were: from Dec's flirty brother Cal, to big, tough Logan.

It was just her luck that she worked with some prime specimens of the male species, and didn't feel a spark with any of them. She frowned. Most days she wondered if she'd ever find the right guy. She was the queen of the first date. She'd been on a long string of them, and rarely had a second one. She just couldn't find a guy who made her melt, and who could keep up with her at the same time. Most guys glimpsed her guns or knives and ran in the opposite direction.

She paused and spotted a guy checking her out. He was staring at her legs. She mentally rolled her eyes. Who needed a guy, anyway? They were all so boring and predictable.

"A drink, Miss?" A waiter paused beside her, holding out a glass of champagne.

Morgan was about to refuse, when she glanced at the waiter again. It took her a second to realize it was Coop. She accepted the glass with a smile, knowing it wouldn't actually be champagne. She tried to work out what he'd done to make himself look different. Padding in his cheeks, maybe? Shaping on his chin?

"Thank you." She took a sip. Sparkling water.

Coop pulled out a cloth and started to wipe a nearby table. He leaned close to her. "Keep flashing that smile and those legs. Every man in the room is watching you."

"They always do," came Dec's dry voice through the earpiece.

Morgan sniffed. She didn't dress up very often, but when she did, she knew she cleaned up pretty well. "Tell me more about this emerald pendant?"

"The Mughal Rulers of India were renowned for their gemstone collections. Especially their carved emeralds. The emerald pendant is hexagonal-cut, just shy of one hundred and fifty carats, and intricately carved with lotus and poppy flowers."

Morgan took another sip of her drink, her gaze falling on the largest pedestal at the front of the room. The emerald pendant was the star of the show.

"We were hired by Dr. Zachariah James," Dec continued. "He's a well-known archeologist and has made a name for himself finding very rare artifacts that were considered lost forever."

Morgan lifted her glass to cover her lips. "A regular Indiana Jones."

"My father speaks very highly of him," Dec said.

Instantly, she imagined Zachariah James to be an older, professor-like man with graying hair. Dec's dad might be a silver fox—fit and gorgeous—

but Morgan was well aware that most historians and archeologists looked nothing like Dr. Oliver Ward.

"The emerald is on display just ahead of you," Dec continued. "It's on an open stand. No covers."

Risky. She headed in that direction, instantly spotting the sparkle of green under the lights. She passed two younger men who were gawking at her, their mouths open. She flashed them a flirtatious smile.

Then she reached the emerald.

"Wow." As she circled the pedestal she didn't need to fake her amazement. The jewel was damn impressive. The large emerald was carved with exquisite flowers and circled by small diamonds. It would fit perfectly in the palm of her hand.

She leaned forward, no longer looking at the emerald. Now she was searching for any sign of the security system—alarm or pressure sensors. Nothing was visible.

"One hundred and forty-two carats. Intricate design of flowers that matches designs you'll find in the Taj Mahal. She's a beauty."

The deep voice, edged with a hint of playfulness, made her look up.

Across the emerald's stand, her gaze collided with a man's. Something inside Morgan went very still.

She sized him up in a second. A few inches over six feet, broad shoulders that filled out his white dress shirt, fit and lean, with tanned skin that suggested he liked the outdoors, and the sharp, handsome face of a fallen angel. He had tawny hair, filled with brown and gold strands, that looked like it was well beyond needing a cut, and green eyes the same shade as the emerald in front of them, which watched her with blatant interest.

Morgan finally found her voice. "It's gorgeous." *A little bit like you.*

He smiled. "I have a weakness for beautiful things."

She fought back the urge to blink. Damn, the man's smile was a weapon. He had straight, white teeth, beautiful lips, and dimples. Morgan was a sucker for dimples.

Pull yourself together, Morgan. She raised a brow and smiled. "Does that line usually work for you?"

He lifted a shoulder. "I've had more luck with it than you'd expect." He extended a hand to encompass the room. "I work here. I helped create this exhibit."

Morgan forced herself to focus on the job and not this man's charm and good looks. "Oh? Well, congratulations. It's a great party. I almost didn't come."

He circled the stand. "Why?"

She shrugged. "My ex got the tickets, and, well…" She waved a hand, falling easily into her character. "There was a messy breakup. I'm sure you don't want to hear all the gory details." She smiled. "I got the tickets for this exhibition, though."

Another sexy smile. "Your ex must be an idiot."

"Now, there is something we can both agree on." She lifted her glass and took a sip. Her gaze fell back on the emerald. "Tell me more about this fabulous gem."

"It was commissioned by the Mughal Court, possibly sometime during the reign of Emperor Shah Jahan. That puts it somewhere in the mid-1600s. Sometime after that, it made its way into the hands of an official of the British East India Company."

Morgan tilted her head. "British East India Company. I've heard of that."

The man nodded. "The English company, along with its fleet of East Indiaman ships and large, private armies, eventually controlled large areas of India and much of the trade of cotton, silk, salt, tea, and opium. The company officials established sprawling estates and helped themselves to much of India's treasures. They laid the groundwork for the British Crown to later step in and assume rule in India."

He lit up as he told her the history. "Fascinating. So how did this emerald end up here?"

"It was transported as part of cargo headed back to England on a ship called the *Verelst*. The ship sank off the coast of Mauritius." That smile again. "My team and I dived the wreck last year, and one of the artifacts we recovered was this incredible gem."

"You dive shipwrecks?"

He nodded. "Underwater archeology is one of my

areas of interest." Suddenly, his gaze moved over her shoulder, and he stiffened. "Hold that thought, and please excuse me for just a moment."

"Sure."

Morgan pretended to fiddle with her hair, and glanced in the direction her private tour guide was looking. He was deep in quiet conversation with a security guard, but his gaze was on a man leaning against the wall.

He'd spotted Declan.

Hmm. So whoever this guy was, he knew that THS had been hired to test the security.

After the guard had moved off in Dec's direction, the man looked back at her and smiled. "Sorry about that."

God, the megawatt smile was panty-melting. The man had it down to a fine art. "No problem. I realize you're working, as well." She turned back to the emerald. "So, is it safe? I can't believe you have an amazing emerald just sitting out here like this."

His face turned a little serious. "We have state-of-the-art security."

"Oh?" Morgan made a big show of looking at the sides of the pedestal.

He laughed and of course, he had a sexy laugh, too. "You can't see anything. There's a special sensor system that picks up body heat that's in close range to the emerald for too long, and triggers an alarm. And a backup."

She arched her head to look at him. "A backup?"

"If someone gets past the first system, then it is also calibrated to the emerald's exact weight. If it's moved off the pedestal, then an alarm is triggered."

"That's impressive."

"Thank you. Do you need a refill?" He gestured at her empty glass.

She shot him a smile and watched his gaze drop to her lips. "I'd love one." She handed her empty glass to him, and their fingers brushed. His gaze flicked back up to hers, locked there. Morgan felt a faint trickle of electricity through her hand, and she blinked.

"What's your name?" he suddenly demanded.

"We're having so much fun, I don't want to tell you and break the spell," she said, only half kidding.

The smile was back. "Okay, Ms. Mysterious. Stay right here, and I'll convince you to tell me when I get back."

Then he was gone, walking through the crowd with a loose-hipped stride that made more than one woman look his way.

Focus, Morgan. She pulled off one of her earrings and peeled off the tiny sensor attached to it. She stepped closer to the pedestal and gently pressed the tiny, transparent dot to the stand. "Dec?"

"Got it. I'm patching you through to Darcy."

"I'm here," came Darcy's melodious voice. Dec's younger sister was sitting several miles away, in the converted warehouse that housed the Treasure Hunter Security offices. Morgan could picture her sitting in front of her wall of screens.

"I'm tapping into the security system now," Darcy said.

"I need to know how much this emerald weighs," Morgan murmured.

"Searching now," Darcy said.

Morgan scanned around the crowd for that tawny head of hair. She spotted him over by the bar. He was a head taller than most of the other people in the room. The bartender was handing him two full glasses. "Hurry it up."

"Fifty-five grams. And the heat sensor will be disabled in three, two, one…"

Coop walked past Morgan, handing her a napkin topped with a few hors d'oeuvres. "Fifty-five grams," he murmured quietly.

Okay, now for the switch. Morgan moved closer to the emerald, looking like she was studying the tiny carvings on the gem. Her heart was beating hard and fast, but she breathed steadily.

She held her left hand up over the emerald and lifted the hors d'oeuvres close with her other.

It was all a matter of timing. And Morgan had excellent timing.

With a quick slide, she skimmed the emerald off as she set the napkin in its place.

Adrenaline flooded her system, but she'd had years of practice controlling it. She took a step back, her fingers closing over the emerald. It felt cool in her hand.

No alarm sounded, and no one converged on her with shouts or screams. She quickly turned, wrapping the emerald in a small cloth she'd brought, and slipping the priceless gem down her neckline, nestling it in her cleavage.

She wandered over to the window, looking at the reflection of the party in the glass.

"Slick." Dec's amused voice.

Morgan hid a smile.

"There you are." Mr. Handsome had returned. He handed her another champagne flute. "Now, I just have to know your name."

Job done, Morgan decided she deserved a drink. She took a large gulp, the champagne fizzing on her tongue. Ugh, she'd much prefer a beer. "You first."

"Dr. Zachariah James."

Morgan choked on the champagne.

Dr. James moved closer, patting a hand to her back. His warm palm hit the bare skin between her shoulder blades. "Hey, take it easy. Did it go down the wrong way?"

She was instantly distracted by the feel of his hand. Skin to skin. Again, she felt that disconcerting tingle where they touched. "I'm fine, Dr. James."

"Please, call me Zach." Up close, she saw golden streaks through the green of his eyes. "Dr. James is so stuffy, and Zachariah is a mouthful."

He straightened, his gaze moving over her shoulder. Then his flirtatious manner disappeared in a blink, his body stiffening. It happened so fast she couldn't quite believe it, and his hard face became nearly unrecognizable.

She turned, following his gaze. He was staring

at the pedestal...and the napkin of hors d'oeuvres resting on top of it.

Dr. James' hands turned to fists at the sides of his rigid body. "Goddammit!"

Chapter Two

Zach James knew most people thought he was a pretty easygoing man, quick to smile and share a laugh.

But that was only because he showed people what he wanted them to see. He'd learned very young to keep his true feelings hidden, or they got used against you. So right now, he let very little of the anger and frustration storming through him show.

He saw the gorgeous woman watching him. She'd caught his eye instantly, with her long, shapely legs and intriguing face with an equally intriguing scar on one cheek. Her short, pixie-cut hair was as dark as ink, her skin bronze, and her eyes the most fascinating aqua blue, just like her tiny dress. He expected to see confusion on her face, but her gaze was impassive, watching him steadily.

Declan Ward sauntered up to them, his hands in the pockets of his trousers. "Evening."

"We were watching you," Zach bit out.

He'd wanted the new security system to work out. He'd helped design it. He hated that visitors to the museum had to view things through inches-thick glass. Zach believed people should be immersed in history and culture, be able to interact and marvel at it. Not that artifacts should be locked away.

But as an archeologist and historian, Zach's first priority was always to safeguard the artifacts.

"I'm not here alone," Declan said.

A waiter appeared just behind Declan. The man gave a single nod, his face grave.

"This is one of my team, Ronin Cooper."

Now that Zach looked at Cooper, he wondered how the hell the guy had ever passed for a waiter. He had broad shoulders, a powerful body, and a look in his dark eyes that was more than a little frightening.

Zach shook his head. "Well, you guys are good." He held his hand out. "I want the emerald back." He'd hired Treasure Hunter Security, but every second the jewel was out of his sight left him twitchy.

Declan shrugged. "I don't have it." He nodded behind Zach. "She does."

Zach turned and his gut tightened. *No way.* The insanely attractive woman he'd been drawn to had a faint smile on her face.

The wide-eyed wonder was gone. She winked, reached down the front of her tight dress, and pulled out the Mughal emerald.

"You were watching me, too," she said. "But you only saw what you wanted to see."

Right. He'd only seen legs up to her ears, and

pouty red lips that had made him think dirty, dirty thoughts. He'd seen a sexy woman who shivered each time he'd touched her.

Now, he saw a dangerous glint in her eyes. There was a lot more to this woman than her good looks. But a part of Zach was angry that her reaction to him might have just been an act.

She handed over the emerald.

Zach took it, ensuring his fingers brushed against her palm. He watched her carefully.

She pulled her hand back quickly, something flashing in her eyes.

He smiled. At least something about her had been the truth. The emerald was warm, and he realized the warmth came from her skin. Hell, from her breasts.

Shit. The last thing he needed now was an erection. "Treasure Hunter Security came highly recommended, but I wanted to be sure." He looked at Declan. "I wanted to see for myself."

Declan raised a brow. "A test?"

"You can call it that," Zach answered. He waved over one of the museum security guards. He passed off the emerald. "Get it back on the display, and set someone to watch it."

"You need our help with museum security?" Declan asked.

"No." He looked at the woman again. "I wouldn't have pegged you for security, Ms...?"

"Then I was doing my job right. And it's Morgan. Morgan Kincaid."

Morgan. It was a strong name, unbending. And

looking at her now, he thought it suited her. But off the job, did she bend for a man? Did she melt under someone's strong hands? "Well, you intrigued me the first moment I saw you. Now I'm even more intrigued."

Morgan raised a brow. "Well, you'd best get un-intrigued, Dr. James."

Oh, no. He didn't plan to do that.

She leaned in closer, lowering her voice. "And you should always remember to expect the unexpected."

Declan cleared his throat, looking amused. "Dr. James, you aren't the first guy to fall for Morgan's charms. That's why we always send her in for these kinds of jobs. Now, if you don't want our help with security for your exhibit, what do you want?"

"I have a job for you," Zach said.

Declan looked at the others, and then back at Zach. "I'm listening."

Zach glanced around the crowded room. "Not here. Let's go to my office."

He led them past a guard and down a long corridor. They crossed the main level of the museum, a giant open room with the skeleton of a giant plesiosaur hanging from the ceiling, and then he turned down another corridor, where the staff offices were located.

His office was a little messy, but that was normal. He knew where everything was, and that was all that mattered. His favorite photo of himself and his expedition team—all in their dive gear and holding up artifacts from the wreck of the *Verelst*—

was on the wall. He was holding the Mughal emerald in his hand.

Zach sat in his battered office chair, while Declan took one of the guest chairs on the other side of the desk. Ronin Cooper leaned against the wall, and Morgan prowled over to his only window. There was only nighttime darkness outside.

God, those legs. It was impossible not to look at them. He saw the strength in them now. Sleek muscles he hadn't noticed before. How he'd mistaken her for a regular woman on a night out, he didn't know. They all watched him expectantly.

Down to business. "Several weeks ago, the museum was given a collection of letters and personal effects of people who were missionaries for the American Lutheran Church. The group worked in Madagascar, and had their headquarters in a former French settlement on the south of the island called Fort Dauphin, nowadays called Tolagnaro." Zach sat back in his chair. "Some of the letters were written by local Malagasy people who'd worked closely with the missionaries, and their ancestors. One letter belonged to a former Malagasy servant, Jean, who had worked for the French Governor of Fort Dauphin in the late 1600s before the French abandoned the settlement." He shot them a thin smile. "Or were forced out by the locals, depending which side you were on."

"So, who is this Jean?" Declan asked.

"Well, we already knew that a Malagasy called Jean had told an interesting story to a rescued French sailor, who then went on to replay the story to the Governor of the French East India Company."

"I take it the French East India Company was in competition with the British East India Company?" Morgan asked.

"You'd be right. Many of the European countries had trading companies and fleets, trying to snag their share of wealth from the East Indies. The Dutch were ahead of the game, with the largest share of the trade, followed by the English. The French East India Company was founded to compete and give the French a slice of the pie."

"And did they get a slice?" Morgan asked.

"A little. But they never reached the levels the Dutch and British did. They did start negotiations with Siam."

"Thailand," Ronin said.

Zach nodded. "It was all thanks to a charismatic Greek adventurer by the name of Constantine Phaulkon helping to broker the deal between France and Siam. He was a fascinating man. A former clerk for the British East India Company, he arrived in Siam as a merchant. In a matter of a few years, he became fluent in Thai, worked in the royal court, and became the number one counselor to King Narai. There were plenty in the king's court who resented the foreigner's fast rise to power, and thought he wielded far too much control." Zach blinked. "Sorry, I'm getting off track." He saw Morgan smirking at him. "I just find Phaulkon so interesting. Anyway, King Narai, hoping to impress the French King—Louis XIV, also known as the Sun King—wanted to send some ambassadors to France, along with some gifts to sweeten the deal. A ship called the *Soleil d'Orient* set sail, and do you want to guess the next part of the story?"

"It never made it to France," Morgan said.

"Correct. Considered lost at sea, or perhaps the Siamese ambassadors set it alight with their incessant smoking."

"So what did this Jean see?" Declan asked.

"He saw the *Soleil d'Orient* limp into Fort Dauphin, leaking badly. The crew befriended the locals as their ship was repaired. When they headed back out, they were caught in a storm, and the ship sank just off the Madagascan coast, north-east of Tolagnaro."

"And no one's ever found it?" Ronin asked.

"No. A few people have tried, but they've never found the wreckage."

Morgan moved closer. "But you have."

Excitement trickled through Zach's veins, the same way it did every time he was on the trail of an historic find. "Yes. Jean didn't share everything with the French. In his papers, we found he'd marked the exact location of where the *Soleil d'Orient* went down. We've kept that information under wraps."

Declan nodded. "No one wants word of an important shipwreck leaking to the wrong people."

"No. The last thing I need is every would-be treasure hunter descending on Madagascar. Treasure Hunter Security is highly recommended, but I need a team with expert underwater recovery skills as well."

Declan smiled. "Most of my team are former Navy SEALs, Dr. James. Except for Morgan. Although she may as well have been."

Zach eyed Morgan, wondering what her background was.

"Navy," she said, answering his unasked question. "And I passed the SEAL training."

Zach's eyes widened. He knew the failure rate was high for BUD/S training. He was impressed. As far as he knew, no woman had officially ever passed it before. He forced his gaze back to Declan. "Can you get a ship suitable for the recovery operation?"

Declan nodded. "Yes. But it's top of the line, and it'll cost you."

Zach's heart began to pound. This was it. He was going to find the *Soleil d'Orient* and her cargo. There was so much history awaiting in the hold of that ship, and possibly any number of secrets kept hidden for years by the waves. He looked at Morgan as she leaned a hip against his desk. He had to admit that having the oh-so-attractive Morgan Kincaid on this expedition would make it even more interesting.

Dr. Zachariah James and team, discoverers of the wreck of the *Soleil d'Orient*. It was a long way from the trailer park he'd grown up in.

He cleared his throat, reality crashing back in for a moment. "My funding won't cover a top-of-the-line ship."

Declan arched a brow. "We don't do charity work, Dr. James."

"I've already got signed salvage deals with the Madagascan government. I'm also willing to pay you a percentage of what we salvage."

Declan crossed his arms over his chest. "It doesn't do my company much good if we find a bunch of rusted cannonballs."

Morgan leaned closer. "What exactly was on that ship, Dr. James?"

Zach vowed to himself that before this expedition was over, he'd get Morgan Kincaid to call him by his first name.

"Treasure, Morgan." He looked at Declan. "A lot of it."

Declan straightened. "Spell it out for me."

"Valuable antiquities, including a golden dinner service the King of Siam had received from the Emperor of Japan, and priceless Chinese porcelain. In addition to that, gold, silver, coins, and chests of diamonds."

Morgan just stared and Ronin gave a low whistle.

Declan's face was impassive for a long moment. Then, he stood. "You've got yourself a security team."

Chapter Three

The winter morning was fresh, and the sky was blue. Snow crunched under Morgan's boots as she strode up the steps to the Treasure Hunter Security warehouse.

There was a spring in her step. She was eager for the hunt. Apart from last night's job at the museum, she hadn't been out in the field for the last few weeks, and she was starting to feel itchy.

She pushed through the glass doors and into the warehouse. Dec had bought the old flour mill and had converted it. He and Layne lived in the spacious upstairs apartment, and the huge, open space below was for the office.

Morgan honestly admitted she loved the space, with its polished concrete floors, exposed brick walls, and large windows offering a good view of the city. The far end housed Darcy's domain. The youngest Ward sibling was something of a computer geek, although she hardly looked like one, and the opposite brick wall was covered in computer screens. Off to one side sat their long conference table, and on the other side, worn couches faced some games tables that they played during their downtime—pool, air hockey, and their latest addition, a foosball table. Morgan played a mean game of table soccer.

Two men were currently locked in a vicious air-hockey battle. Ronin raised a hand, while his opponent shot Morgan a quick smile. Hale Carter was another former SEAL. He was their resident fix-it man in the field. Hale hadn't met an engine or gadget—or woman—he couldn't fix or finesse. With glossy dark skin, a handsome face, and a gorgeous smile, he loved the ladies, and they loved him.

As Morgan headed for the small kitchenette tucked in the back, she heard the click of heels on the floor. She slipped off her leather jacket, slung it over the back of one of the couches, and turned. "Morning."

"Good morning. This new job sounds amazing," Darcy Ward said.

That was Darcy. Straight to the point. Of medium height with a slim build, Darcy always looked like she'd just stepped out of the pages of some fancy fashion magazine. Today, she was wearing dark jeans tucked into knee-high boots, and an emerald-green shirt that contrasted nicely with the dark bob of her hair. She had wide, blue-gray eyes, which were a combination of Dec's gray and Callum's blue.

"It does sound good," Morgan said. "But we have to find it, first. Shipwrecks are notorious for hiding their secrets." Morgan strode over to the small kitchenette, grabbed a mug, and poured herself some coffee from the pot.

"But you have the location of where the ship sank."

Morgan turned, leaning back against the countertop. "Sure. But the final resting place of wrecks are often found miles from where they actually sank. It depends on the currents, the sea floor, other conditions—"

Darcy waved a hand. "Well, Zachariah is very good at what he does."

Morgan stilled and stared at her coffee. "You know him?"

Darcy nodded. "I've met him once or twice." Darcy got a far-off look in her eye, smiling. "He has that whole adventurer-vibe going on. Did you see his smile?"

Morgan sighed. "I sure did. And his dimples."

"Dimples..." Darcy shook her head, like she was clearing it. "He lectures at the University of Denver with Dad. Students fight to get to study with him." Darcy waggled her perfectly shaped brows. "Especially the female students."

Why wasn't Morgan surprised? She sipped her coffee, and noticed a body sprawled on one of the couches. She strode over, sat down, and bumped the sleeping man's hip with her own. "Sleeping on the job, O'Connor?"

The big former SEAL grunted, lifted his boots onto the coffee table, and folded his muscled arms across his chest. "Had a late night."

"Oh? Do anything exciting?"

Logan opened one gold eye and gave her a slow smile. No one would ever call Logan handsome.

With his mountainous body and his rugged face, he had too many jagged edges. But when he smiled, like he did now, it eased all the rough lines. "Pretty certain you don't want me to tell you what Sydney and I were doing last night."

Morgan took a hurried sip of her coffee. "Please don't." That was all Morgan needed—X-rated images of Logan with his oh-so-feminine and stylish fiancée.

Suddenly Logan's face lit up. "Speak of the devil."

Morgan turned her head and saw Sydney Granger striding toward them, holding a stack of files. Tall, slender, and elegant, Sydney wore neat slacks and a shirt in pale pink that had some sort of tie that wrapped around her neck. Her pale-blonde hair was caught up in some effortless-looking twist that Morgan would never be able to do.

Sydney might work for Treasure Hunter Security now, and be engaged to the wild, rugged man beside Morgan, but she still looked like the society woman and former CEO she'd been.

"Hi, Morgan."

"Sydney." Morgan's gaze dropped to the stack of files and she suppressed a shudder. Morgan hated paperwork while Sydney reveled in her job taking care of the business side of THS.

"Morning." Declan strode in, and with a ripple of muscles, pulled a gray sweater over his T-shirt. "I call our planning meeting to order."

Morgan moved toward the conference table,

snorting. "Layne's almost got you housetrained."

Dec gave her a hard stare. "Don't be nasty."

"Where is Layne?"

"Here." The pretty brunette bounced down the stairs leading from the upper level. She was holding a stack of papers and was dressed in slacks and a nice shirt. She was also frowning.

"You look stressed," Morgan said.

"I'm giving a guest lecture with Oliver at DU today." She tucked a strand of hair behind her ear. "Nothing like working with your future father-in-law to give you a case of the nerves."

Dec wrapped an arm around her. "He loves you."

"And he's hot," Morgan added. "In a sexy silver fox way."

Dec pretended to kick her, and they moved to the conference table. Everyone made themselves comfortable, cradling coffee mugs. Logan had snagged what looked like a day-old donut from somewhere. Darcy stepped up beside Dec, holding a slim tablet.

"I've been running searches on the *Soleil d'Orient* all night." Darcy grinned. "I've confirmed that she's a very big catch. I managed to find a copy of her cargo manifest." Some of the screens on the wall filled with information. Morgan could see some photocopies of old documents—manifests, and what looked like old newspaper clippings. Most were in French. Morgan could speak some French, but her reading wasn't great.

"Let me run this through my translation program." Darcy touched something on her tablet.

New text appeared beside each document, in English.

Morgan scanned the list of treasure: antiquities, gold, silver, diamonds.

Logan let out a whistle. "Diamonds as big as a baby's fist. Nice."

His fiancée arched her pale brow. "You've never even been near a baby, and since when do you like diamonds?"

"Since I started watching you wear them." His voice lowered. "Naked in our bed."

Color filled Sydney's cheeks. "Quiet."

"Zachariah requested a ship," Darcy continued on, shooting Logan a narrow-eyed glance. "Dec contacted Diego. He's agreed to join the expedition. He'll meet up with you, with the *Storm Nymph*."

Morgan sat back in her chair. She liked Diego Torres. He was another former SEAL, but one who could never give up his love of the water. He owned a research and salvage vessel, the *Storm Nymph*, which he hired out for underwater archeology and oceanographic expeditions.

"I hate narrow ship bunks," Logan grumbled. "Never fit in them."

Morgan rolled her eyes. Logan always found something to be grumpy about.

Dec turned to face their teammate. "Well, Logan, you'll be happy to hear that the team for this mission will be myself, Morgan, Coop, and Hale."

"I've organized commercial flights for you all," Darcy said. "You'll fly into Mozambique and meet Diego and the *Storm Nymph* at the Port of Maputo.

You'll sail across to Madagascar, and meet Zachariah and his team in Tolagnaro."

There were nods and mumbled acknowledgements.

Sydney cleared her throat, setting her clasped hands on the table. "We need to talk about our *other* project."

Dec scowled. "Go on."

Tension filled the room. Morgan knew exactly what project Sydney was talking about. Silk Road.

The black-market antiquities ring operated in the shadows. They were well-funded, and targeted valuable artifacts and treasures. They were ruthless, and thought nothing of killing to get what they wanted.

Treasure Hunter Security had collided with them a few times. But after they'd kidnapped Sydney's younger brother in South America while on the trail of an ancient treasure, Sydney had made it her mission to bring the group down.

It wasn't an easy task.

"I've had very little luck getting people to talk about Silk Road." Sydney huffed out a breath. "I've had better luck chasing the money. Darcy's been helping me. By narrowing down countries and locations where we know they've been operating, I've been able to trace some payments they've made. Of course, it all leads back to a tangle of offshore companies and accounts." Frustration rose in her voice. "I'm still working on it, but I'm continuing to pull the threads. I'm getting closer."

Darcy stepped forward. "I've also been running

searches for any references to Silk Road, their operations, or their known associates. We're marking those on maps to see if we can find any pattern."

Sydney nodded. "A few things have lined up. I think there may be three main people running things behind the scenes."

"Why?" Morgan asked.

"The money seems to always come in from three different sources. I don't know what or where those sources are, but there are three." A deep sigh. "It's mostly just speculation at this point."

"My searches are still running," Darcy said. "I have a list of their known associates, people they hire. One thing I have noticed is this—"

A screen lit up, showing a map of a city. A familiar city spotted with red dots.

"London's a hotspot," Dec said, his gaze narrowed.

"It appears to be," Darcy confirmed. "But that could just be because of the concentration of museums and private collections to steal from. I'm still working on it."

The screen zoomed out, showing a map of the globe covered in red dots and connecting lines.

Dec nodded. "Good work, both of you. Make sure you don't do anything to tip them off that you're looking at them."

Darcy sniffed. "Please."

"Silk Road has caused too much trouble and too many deaths." Dec's tone darkened. "We'll do whatever we have to do to bring them down." He looked at his sister. "Keep working on it. And whatever you uncover, I need you to coordinate with Agent Burke at the FBI. You know he's investigating these guys as well, and he'll have extra information that could help."

Darcy wrinkled her nose. "I'm only talking to that man if I have to."

Dec made a grumbling sound. "He's the FBI, Darce. You don't get a choice."

Darcy muttered some possibly choice words under her breath.

"What are the odds of Silk Road coming sniffing around our shipwreck?" Morgan asked.

"There's the potential for a lot of treasure, for sure," Dec said. "Thus far, Dr. James has done a good job keeping it under wraps."

"Won't take long for word to get out once we're on site," Coop said.

Darcy cleared her throat. "Something our searches are showing is that Silk Road likes to target expeditions with particularly important artifacts. Anything attached to an interesting myth or legend."

"Adds to their value," Hale said.

"And when Silk Road attacked our jobs, we were dealing with a famous lost oasis, a legendary stone, and the hidden treasure of a lost people," Darcy added.

"So is a gift from one king to another from a few hundred years back interesting enough for them?" Dec asked.

"Dr. James mentioned some Japanese plates and

Chinese porcelain," Morgan said.

"But not legendary artifacts," Dec said. "I can't see anything here that would interest them."

"We can't rule it out, though." This time it was Layne who spoke. "You guys need to be careful over there." Her eyes lingered on her fiancé.

"Let's keep our fingers crossed," Morgan said.

"And our eyes peeled," Hale added.

"No one actually says 'eyes peeled', Hale." Morgan shook her head. "Especially badass, former Navy SEALs."

Hale just shot her a wide smile.

Darcy ignored them. "I'll keep monitoring. If we spot any Silk Road members entering Madagascar, I'll let you know."

More images appeared on the screen, and Morgan was instantly drawn to a headshot of Dr. Zachariah James. It captured his handsome face and carefree grin perfectly.

"Wow," Sydney said. "*That's* Dr. James?"

From across the table, Logan growled.

"I met him at a conference once," Layne said with a wistful sigh. "He is *very* easy on the eyes. And he has this charm..."

"He appeared to be rather taken with Morgan," Dec said.

A rare smile crossed Coop's face. "And her legs."

Morgan scowled at them both across the table. Zachariah James struck her as a roguish adventurer. She was certain he only stuck around until the excitement had passed.

"Well, he is only mortal," Darcy said. "I curse

Morgan on a daily basis for having legs like she does."

"Morgan does have amazing legs," Logan conceded.

Sydney reached over and smacked him in the back of the head good-naturedly.

"How about we leave my legs out of it and find some treasure?" Morgan stood, shoving her chair back. "Or I'll be forced to draw my weapon...or maybe kick someone with my amazing legs."

Darcy slapped a folder on the table. "Your trip is all booked. Have fun."

Chapter Four

Zach walked down a busy street in Tolagnaro, taking in his surroundings.

A sense of history pulsed from the tiny Madagascan seaside town built on a small peninsula beside beautiful blue water. Once, it had been a Malagasy village, a landing point for Portuguese explorers, a French settlement, and now, the modern town of Tolagnaro.

He felt the humidity in the air and smelled the salt of the sea. The street was crowded with people bustling along, doing their business, and nearby palm trees waved in the wind.

He and his team had arrived at Tolagnaro's small airport that morning. They'd ended up beating the Treasure Hunter Security team, which was expected to come into the port on the research vessel at any moment.

Which meant he'd get to see Morgan Kincaid again soon. The thought left a fizz in his blood and a smile on his face. He was excited to see what was hiding under her tough exterior.

He dodged around an older Malagasy lady who was herding two laughing children ahead of her. As he glanced back toward the sea, a tingle ran through his veins.

Any time he walked down an unknown street in a new town, he felt that same sense of exploration and adventure. He breathed deep, pulling that sea-air scent into his lungs. Around him, he heard people speaking in both Malagasy and French. He smelled food frying in the nearby café, and the summer sun was warm on his skin. A wonderful change to Denver's wintery chill.

Oh, yeah, he felt the excitement and anticipation of the hunt. History had always made him feel like this. He'd had none of that growing up. His smile dissolved, his muscles tightening. He'd spent his childhood in a dirty trailer, with no mother, worn clothes, and a drunken father who had very big hands.

There'd been no excitement or adventure. Only fear whenever his father was in a rage, and resignation when he'd had to go to school with holes in his shirt.

The only bright spot had been when he'd opened a library book. He felt his shoulders loosen, the tension beginning to ease away. Reading about different ancient kingdoms, warriors, and cultures had been his escape. For those few precious moments, he'd been an Egyptian pharaoh, a Roman centurion, a Chinese emperor, a Portuguese explorer.

Now, history was his life. His gaze moved to the crystal-blue water in the bay. Out there, somewhere, the *Soleil d'Orient* and her treasure were waiting.

He couldn't wait to uncover her story and history.

Someone brushed up against him. "Dr. James?"

One of his graduate students. Charity was a pretty young woman, with long, blonde hair she kept up in a high ponytail, and a curvy, young body. She brushed up against him again.

"I'm *so* grateful to be here. To be a part of this expedition. I want you to know I'll work very hard to make this expedition a success." She shot him a megawatt smile, rubbing her breast against his arm. "I'll do anything that's required."

Zach barely stopped himself from rolling his eyes. He was used to pretty young things flexing their flirting wings. They were all still working out who they were and growing into their sexuality.

He'd learned to dodge like a pro.

He patted Charity's shoulder. She was a smart girl and a hard worker. Those were the things he wanted from her. "We'll all be working hard. We'll have multiple dives every day, in addition to cleaning and examining any artifacts we bring up." He purposely stepped away, and turned to look at the other student with them. "I know the entire team will do their best."

As the two young women nodded and murmured, he saw Charity's shoulders sag.

They moved on down the street, Charity striding ahead. She had a shiny new camera hanging over one shoulder and a bulging backpack on the other.

He shook his head. He'd have to have another

talk with the group about being careful with what they flashed around in countries where people didn't always have as much. His archeologists were experienced and used to traveling in foreign countries, but some of these students hadn't ventured far from home before.

Suddenly, someone rushed past Zach, bumping into him. The young local man grabbed the strap of Charity's camera and yanked it off her. She let out a short scream, and the thief grabbed her backpack, as well.

"Stop!" Charity yelled. "All my things!"

Zach lunged forward, but the man was fast, shooting off down the sidewalk.

All of a sudden, an arm shot out and slammed into the thief's chest. The man was knocked back a step. With two hard hits, their rescuer brought the thief to his knees. He dropped the bag and camera and knelt on the ground, wheezing.

Morgan Kincaid leaned down and grabbed the stolen items. She paused to whisper something in French to the thief.

The man nodded jerkily, shot to his feet, then ran off, fear written all over his face.

Morgan straightened. Dark sunglasses hid her aqua-blue eyes, but Zach swore he could almost *feel* her assessing gaze. Damn, she looked amazing. Her fantastic legs weren't in view, covered in khaki cargo pants, and she wore a simple tight, black T-shirt that showed off her firm breasts and toned arms.

But, it was that edgy face with the faint scar

that got to him. She wasn't quite beautiful, but she was sure as hell attractive.

She held the backpack and camera out to Charity. "I believe these are yours?"

"Thank you so much." Charity clutched the bag to her chest. "It happened so fast."

Morgan tilted her head. "It's best to keep the expensive stuff out of sight in your bag. And make sure you've got both straps of your backpack on your shoulders. Stay focused on your surroundings." Morgan's tone was as dry as dust, her gaze moving to meet Zach's.

Great, so she'd seen Charity's amateur flirting.

"Dr. James," Morgan said.

"Morgan. It's a pleasure to see you again." He stepped closer, smiling. She was only a couple of inches shorter than him, and he liked that.

Out of the corner of his eye, he saw Charity's gaze sharpen on them. Her shoulders drooped again.

"Where is the rest of your group?" Morgan asked.

"Eating at a local café. They're taking care of our luggage, as well. We thought we'd have a look around." He turned to look at his students. "Charity and Jasmin, I'd like to introduce you to Morgan Kincaid. She's part of our security team."

Morgan shook hands with the students. "Great to meet you. Now, if you're ready, the ship is waiting and we should collect the rest of your team." She looked at Zach again. "I'm sure you're eager to get started."

The students moved ahead, and Zach fell into step with Morgan, matching his stride to hers. "Do you enjoy diving?"

"I love it."

"I'm looking forward to finding out what else you love."

She shot him a small grin. "If you're waiting for me to bat my eyelashes at you like Blondie did, you'll be waiting a long time."

"Charity is harmless. And I prefer women. Smart, strong women."

Morgan shook her head. "Watch it, Dr. James. One thing I do love is my gun collection, followed by my knife collection."

Fascinating woman. "I enjoy collecting, as well. Artifacts. I'll show you mine if you show me yours?"

Now she snorted.

"Ah. Here we are," Zach announced.

Before them sat the café, and he spotted his two archeologists and third student sitting at an outdoor table. Duffel bags and hard cases containing their gear formed a small mountain beside them.

Morgan flicked open a sleek, black phone and tapped something in.

"Everyone, I'd like to introduce Morgan Kincaid from Treasure Hunter Security," Zach said. "Morgan, this is Dr. Alice Still and Dr. Taye Duncan." He gestured to each of his team members.

Alice was a fit Australian woman in her forties, with auburn hair pulled tightly back in a braid. She was an experienced field archeologist and diver. Taye was a slender man with dark skin and a shaved head. He had a knack for restoring artifacts, and he and Zach had been friends for years.

"And this is our third grad student, Max." The young man looked a little awe-struck as he shook Morgan's hand.

She nodded her head at them. "We're all looking forward to this expedition, and the *Storm Nymph* is waiting for us at Port d'Ehoala. It's about five miles out of Tolagnaro."

Just then, three silver SUVs pulled up. Zach watched Ronin Cooper slide out of the lead vehicle. A good-looking, broad-shouldered, African-American man got out of the second. He went back and tipped a Malagasy man who'd been driving the third.

"This is our ride," Morgan said, hefting up two of the cases. "Everyone meet Ronin Cooper and Hale Carter."

Zach felt an unfamiliar and very uncharacteristic stab of jealousy. Morgan worked daily with these tough men. Was she attached to any of them?

As his team moved forward to help load the bags into the SUVs, Zach grabbed Morgan's arm. "Back at the museum, that story you told about your ex, that wasn't true, was it?"

"No."

"So, there isn't really a boyfriend?"

An arched brow. "None of your business, Dr. James."

He stared at her face for a second, then let her go. Satisfaction flooded him. "If there was, you would have thrown it in my face." He smiled. "Good."

She rolled her eyes. "Dr. James—"

"Zach."

Her jaw tightened. "Dr.—"

He leaned in close. "We're going to be spending a lot of time together, Morgan. You may as well use my name."

"Dr. James, we're here to work. That's it. I don't get involved with clients, and I have a job to do."

Zach leaned closer. He'd learned from a young age to fight for what he wanted. If you gave up at the first sign of trouble, you got nowhere.

"I like adventure, Morgan, and I like a challenge. I've made it my motto to pack as much of it as possible into life." He winked at her, sliding into the passenger seat of her SUV. "I think I'll grow on you."

She shook her head. "Like an annoying rash?" She slammed the door shut, and Zach laughed.

* * *

"Welcome to Port d'Ehoala," Morgan said, as she turned the SUV into the port.

In contrast to Tolagnaro, the tiny port was quite new. Arching gracefully out through the water, an artificial breakwater wall protected the port. There was one quay with three berths for ships, two smaller and one large.

She knew that most of the infrastructure had been built by a large mining company that had an ilmenite mine in the area, but the port also serviced container ships and cruise liners. There were a few large warehouses, and a fenced area containing some stacked shipping containers.

Morgan glanced at Zach and saw his gaze had zeroed in on the *Storm Nymph,* where she sat beside the quay. In the backseat, the two female students were pressed up against the windows, staring with interest at their surroundings.

Zach looked comfortable in his outdoor gear and his scuffed boots. She always looked at people's shoes to get their measure. He didn't sit behind a desk all day. He looked just as handsome in the sunshine as he did at night. And maybe she liked him better in cargo pants than she did in his slick suit. The sun turned the light strands in his hair gold, and he radiated an energy that she could almost feel on her skin.

"She's a beauty," Zach said.

Diego's research vessel wasn't the largest, but she had everything a good science and salvage ship needed: high-tech communications, research labs, staging spaces, cranes, and submersible ROVs.

She spotted Dec leaning against the railing at the top of the ramp. She pulled the SUV to a stop behind Hale's.

Soon, she was striding up the ramp to the ship, Zach a step behind her.

"Nice to see you again, Declan." Zach held out a hand.

"You too, Dr. James."

"Please, call me Zach. Morgan refuses to."

A faint smile crossed Dec's face. "She's stubborn."

"And standing right here," she grumbled.

A man appeared above, on the balcony surrounding the bridge. He came down the stairs in smooth, easy movements that said he'd done it a hundred times before.

His dark hair was even shaggier than Zach's, his skin tanned a deep brown, and he had scruff on his face. If there was ever a man who looked more like a sexy, salty man of the sea, she'd never seen him.

"And here comes our captain now." Morgan grinned at Diego. He still had the hard body of a SEAL, but ragged cutoff shorts and a dark T-shirt were now his uniform. Tattoos peeked out from under one sleeve, and terrible scars graced the other arm. "Everyone, this is Captain Diego Torres."

"Dr. Zach James." With confident ease, Zach brushed by her to shake Diego's hand.

"Welcome aboard. Looking forward to this expedition." Diego's voice was deep, with a slight southern twang. "I'm excited to help you find the *Soleil d'Orient.* I've heard stories about that wreck over the years. No one's had any luck finding her."

"I'm a pretty lucky guy," Zach said.

Diego inclined his head. "Yeah, I heard about when you found the *Verelst.*"

"You have a great ship. She's perfect for the job."

Diego's dark gaze swept over his ship

affectionately. "The *Nymph* is the only woman I need." The man's face turned serious. "Should we expect any trouble?"

"When there's treasure involved, I always expect trouble," Zach said. "That's why we have Dec and his team with us. We have agreements in place with the government, and I've been communicating with a local Madagascan archeologist for several months now. He's an expert on local history, and he's briefed me on everything he knows."

Morgan saw Zach's team coming up the ramp, carrying all their bags. "Let's get your guys settled."

"After that, I'd like a tour," Zach said.

"Sure." *Great.* Just what she wanted to do. Be stuck in tight confines with him.

"Keep an eye out for my crew," Diego said. "Marc and Turner. Father and son."

As Zach's team boarded, introductions were made, then Morgan led the archeologists and students down into the main cabin area. "Bridge is up top, then the level beneath that is the galley. On this level, you'll find the wet and dry labs, and the computer room." She wrinkled her nose. "Although *room* is probably stretching it. It's more like a cupboard filled with computers. Below the main deck level are the cabins. Of course, the sleeping areas are nice and cozy."

"I assume that means tiny," Charity called out.

"My guys are used to roughing it," Zach said. "This'll still feel like luxury."

"The students will be sharing the larger cabin,"

Morgan said. "There are bunk beds in there. Archeologists each have their own cabins."

"Let me guess," Zach said. "The cabins are cozy."

She flashed him a smile. "You are a perceptive man, Dr. James."

She showed everyone to their assigned cabins, until it was just her and Zach in the tight corridor.

"This is you." She swung the narrow door open.

He leaned in close, his body brushing hers. "Thanks."

Sparks skittered along her arms, and Morgan gritted her teeth. When had the simple brush of a man's body ever affected her like this?

Inside, the small cabin was neat, with a bunk on one side, and a small desk and cupboard on the other. Zach dumped his duffel bag on the bunk.

"Where's your cabin?" he asked.

She raised a brow. "Staff cabins are a bit farther along."

He gestured toward the hallway. "Shall we take that tour now?"

"You're the boss."

They moved back through the hall, and Zach bellowed at his team that they'd meet upstairs in the galley in an hour. She watched him move up the steps ahead of her, her gaze level with his tight ass. It was a work of art.

Morgan huffed out a breath. Jeez, she really needed to get a grip. So the guy was attractive? She'd seen plenty of attractive guys before.

There was no way in hell she was going to tangle with Mr. Charming Adventurer Zachariah James, no matter how delicious every single part of him turned out to be.

Chapter Five

Morgan bypassed the galley, guessing that Zach would want to see the research parts of the ship more than where they were going to eat. They moved into the wet lab.

"This is perfect." He looked at the benches, and the neat storage compartments lining the wall. There were large sinks for washing down artifacts. "This is just what we need to study and store any artifacts that we bring up."

With a nod, she led him through an adjoining door into the dry lab. They did a quick tour, before she led him into the neat-and-tidy galley and dining room.

"Wow." Zach's gaze locked on the large framed painting on the wall.

"It's called *The Cave of the Storm Nymphs*," Morgan told him. "Diego named the ship after it."

The oil painting showed three naked nymphs in a treasure-filled cave, the stormy sea and a foundering ship beyond. The beautiful sirens were caressing the treasure and waiting to lure more sailors to their deaths.

"It's stunning," Zach said.

"Only Diego would name his ship after women

who kill sailors."

Next, Morgan led him back out and down onto the main working deck at the back of the ship. It was filled with various bits of equipment.

"The main crane is for lifting the ROVs in and out of the water. It has a twelve-ton capacity." She pointed at the large yellow crane that was currently tucked into the side of the ship. "ROVs. Large, medium and small depending on the job." The remotely operated underwater vehicles were all tucked securely into racks and locked down. No one wanted expensive equipment flying overboard in rough weather. There was a large ROV, with several attachments at the front for salvage. The smaller units were for relaying camera feed.

Zach stroked a hand over one of the ROVs, and looked like he was staring at treasure. Much like the nymphs in the painting had looked.

Morgan shook her head. Archeologists were the strangest lot. She led him to the very back of the ship. "Here's the A-frame for lifting up anything really heavy." It was actually shaped more like a U and the arm could be lowered down into the water at the back of the ship. Right now, the arm was upright.

She turned to look back at the *Storm Nymph*. The deck was scrubbed clean, and everything stored neatly in its proper place. Diego wouldn't stand for anything else.

"And of course, this is our dive gear." She led Zach over to several SCUBA tanks stacked on a rack. Beside them, compartments were filled with wet suits, buoyancy control device jackets, masks, and fins.

"Top of the line, as promised," Zach said.

"Well, this is pretty standard dive gear. There is some pretty fancy stuff out there nowadays."

"Stuff archeological dig budgets don't cover."

"Right. Or the military keep to themselves."

The two of them ended up at the railing, looking back toward the port. She watched as he drew a deep breath, and then shifted his gaze to look out across the water to the northeast. "She's out there."

She felt the excitement throbbing off him. "If I didn't know better, I'd say this was your first dive."

He smiled at her, his grin making his handsome face look young, playful. "I've dived loads of wrecks, but I've wanted this particular ship for a long time."

She pegged him as an adventurer, always looking for the next shiny thing. "This means a lot to you."

"I've spent years scouring for every bit of information about the *Soleil d'Orient.* Yes, I want her more than anything. I want to bring her history up into the light and share it with the world. Nothing should stay buried and lost in the dark."

Morgan leaned against the railing, a frown tugging at her lips. There was something buried in his voice she couldn't quite place. But the one thing she could easily glean from him was his passion for his work. She loved her job, but she didn't think it left her with the glint she saw in Zach's green eyes.

Suddenly, she felt a touch at her hip, and

glanced down to see Zach looking at the knife sheath she had attached to her belt.

"Hey." She slapped his hand away.

He grinned at her. "How many other weapons do you have hidden on you?"

She scowled at him. He looked intrigued. Most guys were intimidated by her love of sharp objects and projectile weapons. "A lot. You keep touching me without permission, and you'll find out."

His smile widened but he held his palms up, like he was under arrest.

She shook her head. He was incorrigible. She looked back toward the port, and then she frowned. A small group was watching the ship. The people all looked like locals, and she chalked it up to normal curiosity when there was a strange ship in port.

Her gaze moved along the shore, and she spotted another man. He was leaning against some shipping containers, and didn't appear to be paying the ship any extra attention, but Morgan's instincts flared.

"What is it?" Zach started to turn.

"No." She grabbed him, yanking him in close to her body, like they were sharing an intimate moment. She wrapped her arms around Zach's shoulders, turning him a little, so she could look over his shoulder. To the onlookers on the shore, they would appear to be a couple sharing an embrace.

"Morgan, if you wanted to get your arms around me, you just had to ask."

She flicked her gaze back to his. "You can shelve the charm, Dr. James. It's wasted on me."

He tilted his head, his intense green gaze moving over her face. Morgan fought the urge to fidget.

"Really?" he murmured. "Is that because you don't enjoy being charmed, or no one's ever bothered to get past your prickly exterior and try?"

His words made her heart knock against her ribs. How the hell did this man keep getting to her with just a few words? She cleared her throat. "There's a man watching from the shore."

Zach knew instantly what she was doing, and wrapped his arms around her, his lips tickling her ear. "There is a whole crowd of people watching."

God, he was so close. She could feel every inch of his hard body, and it was making it hard for her to concentrate. She arched her neck back to look at him. "I'm not concerned about the crowd. I am concerned about the guy standing off to the side, next to the shipping containers. He doesn't look like an ordinary local. My guess is, he's a pro." She looked Zach straight in the eye. "Why would someone be extra-interested in this dive, Dr. James?"

He let out a large sigh. "I'll get you to call me Zach if it kills me. You're thinking word of the wreck and the treasure's gotten out?"

Maybe that was all it was, but Morgan's gut was warning her that there was something else going on here, and she'd learned long ago to pay attention to her instincts. She needed to run it past Dec.

"Maybe. Any other reason someone would be interested in the *Soleil d'Orient?*"

There was the briefest flicker of something in his eyes, then it was gone. A charming smile crossed his face. "Not that I can think of."

Her gaze narrowed. "You aren't keeping secrets, are you, Doc?"

"You're welcome to strip me bare and check."

She glanced back to the shore and saw the man was gone. She stepped back from the very tempting Zach. "It seems you have a harem of pretty students who would be more than happy to do that."

His face turned serious in a blink. "I've never messed around with my students. Ever. I'm in a position of trust, and I'm here to help them learn."

She nodded. "Right. Sorry. And I never mess around with my clients." She turned to head back to the bridge.

"There's one big difference," Zach said.

Morgan paused and glanced over her shoulder. "Oh?"

"We are two consenting adults." He shot her his trademark smile, sexy dimples flashing. "And you want me."

Infuriating man. Morgan turned and stomped away.

***

The next morning, Morgan stood on the bridge of the *Storm Nymph*, surrounded by the ship's high-tech controls. The bridge was on the top level, with windows all around that allowed for an excellent view in all directions. The main controls were at the front, and in the center of the space was a large table bolted to the floor. Its top was actually a computer screen, and right now the screen was covered in electronic maps.

Dec, Diego, Zach, Dr. Still, and Morgan all stood around it.

"This is the location I've pinpointed from the description listed in Jean's letters." As a glowing dot appeared on the map, off the coast northeast of Tolagnaro, Zach leaned forward, pressing his muscled arms against the edge of the table. As he moved, Morgan watched the flex of his forearms. They were dusted with a light sprinkle of golden hair.

Morgan, get a grip. She purposely focused on the table.

"It's not too deep there," Diego noted. "Around twenty meters."

"Easy diving," Alice Still commented.

Diego nodded. "But this point here, Itapere, has a few reefs, so we'll have to steer clear of those."

"A few ships have floundered at Itapere," Zach said.

"Luckily your ship wasn't farther offshore," Diego added. "Go a few kilometers out, and the sea floor drops sharply. Over a thousand meters, and keeps on going."

"I think we should survey the area with the ROVs first," Dec suggested.

Everyone nodded. Morgan knew it made sense to pinpoint locations with the ROV before they put divers in the water.

"Winds can pick up at that location and the seas can get rough very quickly." Diego looked thoughtful. "We'll have to keep a close eye on the weather."

Zach nodded. "So, we'll get the ROV in the water as soon as possible, do a site scan, and see if we can find our wreckage."

As the men talked more about logistics and search plans, Morgan leaned back against a panel and watched Zach. Right now, he looked nothing like the man who'd been pouring on the charm the day before. His face was serious, his brow furrowed, as he listened to Diego. This was another side of him. The serious, studious archeologist.

Finally, Diego straightened. "All right. Let's go."

As Diego touched the controls of the *Storm Nymph*, he pulled out a handheld radio and instructed his crew to cast off from the wharf. Soon, the ship's powerful engines rumbled to life, the throb vibrating beneath Morgan's feet.

She followed Dec, Zach, and Dr. Still down to the main deck. The students and archeologists were huddled together at the railing, excited.

Zach watched his team with a smile, lifting his face to the sky as the ship sailed out of the harbor. "God, this is the best bit. That moment when all the discovery is ahead of you, and anything is possible." He glanced her way. "Don't tell me you don't enjoy it."

"I do. But part of my job is to foresee the possible troubles. And I know just how much of this is going to be hard, tiring work."

He grinned. "I like the hard work, too. It's all worth it for the chance to hold a piece of history in my hand."

"The past is just the past. Sometimes it's better left there." She thought of her dad, and felt that all-too-familiar pain that refused to fade. It was an ache in her chest that never went away.

Zach's smile dissolved. He reached out, his fingers brushing her jaw. "I get that some things are better left forgotten. Believe me, I do. But putting the pieces back together, rediscovering something for others to learn from and appreciate...that's pretty darn exhilarating."

"That's pretty poetic for an archeologist."

"You want me to quote you poetry?"

Her eyebrows winged up. "Do I look like the poetry kind of girl?"

His sexy dimples flashed. "Hell, no."

The ship moved past the breakwater, and turned northeast. As they moved through the water, the students pointed back to the shore, noting various landmarks. They passed Tolagnaro and the town's pretty curve of white beach. Ahead, the rocky point called Itapere became visible.

"I can almost picture this place around the time when the *Soleil d'Orient* limped in," Zach said. "There would have been ships anchored off shore here, with elegant wooden hulls, three masts, and white sails flapping in the wind."

He had a way with words. Morgan could almost picture the ships on the water.

"But I like to wonder what it might have been like here even earlier than that. When the island was first settled."

She turned her head. "The really ancient stuff floats your boat?"

He nodded. "Underwater archeology is a passion of mine, but my other area of expertise is prehistory, especially megalithic construction."

"Oh?" She instantly imagined giant standing stones. "Like Stonehenge?"

"There is evidence of megalithic construction all over the world, mainly during the Neolithic period. Stonehenge is just the most famous."

"I've always wondered what inspired ancient cultures, who had limited tools and no technology, to lug giant rocks around," she said.

"Who said they didn't have technology?"

She blinked at him. "Huh?"

"We only have theories on how many of the megalithic structures were built, and some are way out there. Some people like to think the ancient cultures had some sort of tech that helped them shape and move the stones."

"From the aliens?" she asked archly.

A quick grin. "Now, no need to go that far. Over the last year, I've combined my love of underwater archeology and megalithic construction. I've been diving sites that are flooded, on the seafloor. Most of them would have been above water a very long time ago. Maybe far enough back to disrupt some established historical timelines. Who knows what they had that's been long lost under the waves?"

Morgan gasped. "You're not talking about Atlantis, are you?"

He shook his head. "I think Atlantis is an amalgamation of myths and legends all polluted with a large dose of fantasy and whimsy."

"It would be pretty out there for a renowned archeologist to study Atlantis."

"You bet," he agreed. "I don't deal in myths, I deal in facts. There's a lot more study to do in this area. I've done a lot of research on prehistoric cultures, flood myths and legends that have been passed down across the globe, and dived some amazing submerged ruins. My last dive was off the south coast of India. About five kilometers off the small fishing village of Poompuhur is a strange, U-shaped structure on the seafloor. It definitely looks manmade."

She nodded. "I dived the Yonaguni Monument in Japan a few years back."

His eyes lit up. "Fascinating place. Did you think it was manmade?"

"Most people think it could be natural...but the giant stones certainly looked too straight and square to me."

Suddenly, the timbre of the engines changed, and the *Storm Nymph* slowed.

Diego and Dec appeared, leaping down the stairs leading from the bridge.

"Time to get Poseidon in the water," Diego said.

Morgan watched as Diego and the two men on

his crew moved over to unlock a small ROV from the rack. Marc was a burly former sailor, and his son, Turner, was a younger, less-grizzled version of his father. Soon, Diego was operating the crane controls, moving the arm over the side of the ship to lower Poseidon into the water.

She watched the boxy, yellow machine disappear into the blue water.

Soon, they were all huddled around Diego's screen, as the ROV moved through the water. Morgan caught glimpses of colorful fish, rocks, and sand.

"We'll start moving in the search pattern," Diego said, tapping the controls. "I'll also run a scan and we can analyze the results later."

And this was where the truth of archeology kicked in. As the ROV methodically moved through the water, no wreck appeared out of the depths. Instead, the search was long and tedious.

After an hour, they'd found nothing.

"You're sure we're at the right coordinates?" Charity asked.

"Yes." Zach didn't look away from the screen. "This takes time. With the tides, shifting sands, storms...a lot has changed down there from when the *Soleil d'Orient* sank."

More time passed, and Diego's hands stayed calm and steady on the controls. Zach's focus never wavered.

Morgan wasn't sure she was comfortable seeing more of the real, genuine man under the charming exterior.

Zach looked at the discouraged faces of his team. "It's pretty rare to find what you're looking for on the first day. A good archeologist needs some patience."

The students peppered him with questions, and he answered them all thoroughly and patiently.

Morgan leaned over Zach's shoulder, staring at the watery image of the seafloor. Clumps of rock littered the sandy ground. A fish swam right up to the ROV before darting off.

"Batteries are running low," Diego said. "Another few minutes, and I'll bring it up."

Morgan stared at a long, elongated rock on the screen. Well, no one could deny that there were plenty of rocks and endless piles of sand. Maybe a secret part of her had expected to see a broken mast, or the rotting hull of the ship. But she knew that underwater archeology wasn't like Hollywood movies.

Then she frowned, studying the long rock again. It was cylindrical in shape, with some sea growth on it.

Then she froze. She knew what it was. She elbowed Zach. "Hey, take a look at this."

He leaned his body against hers as he stared at the screen. Then he sucked in a sharp breath.

"Is that what I think it is?" she asked, excitement licking her insides.

Zach spun around, yanked her close, and smacked a quick kiss on her lips. "That is the cannon off a ship."

The students and archeologists erupted in

cheers. Diego had a faint smile on his rugged face.

Zach smiled at Morgan. "We just found ourselves a shipwreck."

Chapter Six

Zach stepped out on deck and into the early-morning sun. The weather was clear and he'd slept well, even though he'd been buzzing with energy. They'd spent the rest of yesterday afternoon sending the ROV down for more survey runs and scans.

They'd spotted a few more potential artifacts, but they wouldn't know for certain until they got down there.

As he headed down onto the main deck, he saw that Charity and Jasmin were already up. Charity was wearing a bright-pink bikini, while the dark-haired Jasmin had on a floral one-piece swimsuit. He could feel the excitement buzzing around them.

Then he looked up and spotted Morgan checking dive equipment.

Hell. The last thing he needed before he went diving was an erection.

She'd already pulled a wet suit on her bottom half, and on the top half, all she was wearing was a simple black bikini top. She was tanned and toned. His gaze lingered on a set of tight abs that he really wanted to touch.

Zach had always liked women of all shapes and

sizes: curvy, slim, soft, firm. But he'd never wanted to touch a woman as much as he wanted to touch Morgan Kincaid.

She checked some tanks before laying them out on the deck beside a set of fins. He must have made some sort of noise, because she looked up at him.

"Good morning."

"Morning, Morgan."

"Sleep well?"

"Sure did. I'm eager to get in the water."

Morgan turned her head, looking at the water. "Me, too. It's been too long since I was in the ocean."

Zach helped to grab some tanks and gear, and laid everything out neatly on the deck. "Tell me about BUD/S."

"Basic Underwater Demolition/SEAL school. The hardest twenty-four weeks of my life. They push you to the limit. They're testing not just your physical stamina, but mental as well." She shook her head. "A lot of it is a blur of being wet, cold and hurting." A small smile crossed her lips.

He sensed her pride. "But you made it?"

"Sure did."

"The first woman to make it."

She shrugged a shoulder. "I'm stubborn like that. All my life, my dad took me camping, hunting, swimming in freezing-cold lakes. He'd tell me that no kid of his would be a wimp."

Sounded like she was the son her father never had. "He was in the Navy, too?"

She shook her head with a smile. "Marine to the

bone." Sadness moved in her eyes.

Zach understood straightaway. "You lost him."

Her smile vanished. "Yes."

There was a story there, but a story for another day. "Mine's gone, too." *Thank God.* "So what happened after BUD/S?"

"The Navy refused to let me join a SEAL team, so I left."

"And the Navy's screwup is my gain." Declan's deep voice.

Zach looked over at the other man. He was already suited up, a wet suit stretching across his powerful chest and weight belt around his trim waist. Zach pulled on his own suit, and looked over to check that his archeologists and students were almost ready. The first dive would be himself, Alice, Charity and Max.

"Shall we dive?" he asked.

Everyone pulled on their tanks, fins, and masks. Soon, he was sitting on the edge of the boat as Morgan paired everyone up with a dive buddy.

She sat down beside him. "You're with me, doc."

He grinned. *Good.* He pulled his mask over his face, and then let himself roll backward into the water.

Zach hit with a splash, sinking, and waiting for the bubbles around him to fade. He took a second to orient himself, grabbed the control for his BCD and submerged beneath the waves.

Diving always made him feel like he was entering his own little world.

The mask on his face, the sound of his

breathing, the constriction of the wet suit...it all trapped a person in his own little space. But then he looked up and into the clear water ahead, and beyond his little world was an amazing universe.

The water temperature was good and the visibility was great. Conditions were perfect for a successful dive. Now they just had to find what they were looking for.

With a graceful splash, Morgan appeared in the water beside him. She took half a second to right herself, looking sleek and experienced. She paused to tap the waterproof screen attached to her wrist. She had the map marked on there.

He kicked to move forward, and for a second, with the tanks on his back, the weight belt around his waist, and the huge fins, he felt awkward. Morgan looked up and pointed ahead. With two powerful kicks, she was sliding through the water with a grace he'd never match.

Zach kicked again, and just like that, he felt weightless and fluid. That was the beauty of diving. When you forgot about the gear that was there to make an inhospitable environment survivable and simply looked around, it was amazing.

As he followed Morgan, he checked on his students and made sure everyone was following along. Dec was swimming with Alice, and keeping a close eye on the students.

Knowing his team was well looked after, he looked ahead and took his time to admire Morgan's long, lean body.

She looked completely at home in the water. It

was then he noticed that she held a spear gun lightly at her side. Strong, sexy, and dangerous.

Zach's gut tightened. For the first time in his life, he found a woman equally as exciting as his job.

But when Morgan pointed ahead, he jerked his attention off of her and back onto the job.

When she stopped, tapping her screen, he realized they must be at the location of the cannon. He directed his team to start searching. Alice pulled out an underwater camera and started taking some shots.

As the archeologists fanned out, he scanned the seafloor. Seconds later, he spotted the cannon. He grinned around his regulator. As he started taking measurements, he was vaguely aware of Alice floating around him, taking photos. They'd need to bring this beauty up and clean it before they could determine if it was off the *Soleil d'Orient*. Other ships had sunk around this point, so he couldn't be sure just by looking at it half buried in the sand.

He felt a tap on his leg and looked over to see Morgan. She was pointing at the sand nearby. With a few kicks, he joined her, and saw what she was pointing at.

There was a large shard of what looked like porcelain buried in the sand. He moved closer, hoping to make out its pattern. But it was encrusted and covered in muck. From the shape, it was some sort of vase.

He waved Alice over and she took some pictures. He gestured for Charity to extract the piece. As the young woman carefully got to work, Zach pulled a soft net bag off his belt and shook it open. Soon, Charity had eased the item free. Zach's heart kicked. It was, indeed, a vase, and more importantly, it was intact.

They carefully put it in the bag, and he attached it to Charity's dive belt.

They kept searching, fanning out over the area. Max signaled him, and he moved over and found another vase.

This was it. He was sure of it. It had to be the *Soleil d'Orient*. They had no conclusive evidence yet, and this certainly wasn't the main part of the ship, but she was here somewhere.

His head buzzed, his thoughts running rampant, imagining doing a site survey, laying out an artifact grid, running a magnetometer over the site.

Zach floated in the water for a second, adjusting his flotation device. He needed some proof that this was the right ship, and he knew that would take time. He needed to dredge up some of that patience he'd lectured his students about.

But with the possibility of treasure under here, maybe right under his feet, he didn't have a hell of a lot of time. He knew the lure of gold and diamonds would have treasure hunters on top of them in an instant.

He watched Morgan swimming nearby, searching the sand. She'd take time, too. She had a prickly exterior, but something told Zach that if he took his time with her, whatever she hid under that tough shell would be worth the wait.

***

Morgan gripped the edge of the ship and pulled herself up onto the *Storm Nymph*. She carefully set down the soft bag she was carrying, loaded with several artifacts.

Behind her, the others were climbing on board. They were all excited, buzzing and chattering. Everyone started to shed their tanks and gear.

Morgan pulled her mask off and looked around with a frown. Where were Coop and Hale? Where were Diego and his guys? She shook her head. *Slackers.*

After taking off her tank and peeling off her wet suit, she helped the others, setting the tanks back in the racks to be refilled. She grabbed a towel off the pile left on deck and pulled her shorts on.

She turned and got the perfect view of Zach as he stripped off his suit. He wasn't quite as muscular as her colleagues, but there were a lot of lean muscles to appreciate. Her mouth went dry. Lots of lean, well-defined muscles.

"Where the hell are Coop and Hale?" Dec grumbled.

"And Marc and Turner should be getting this gear prepped again for the next dive." Morgan looked across the ship again. It was quiet. Too quiet. "Something's wrong."

Dec snapped into action, pulling his handgun from the stash of clothes he'd left on the deck.

Morgan did the same, settling her SIG Sauer comfortably in her palm.

"What's going on?" Zach asked.

Morgan faced him. "We're not sure. Stay here with your people. Dec and I will take a look around."

Working together, guns up, she and Dec cleared the main deck. There was no sign of the crew or their team members.

"Zach, stay here with your team and do not move," Dec said. "We'll find the others."

Zach nodded, his gaze meeting Morgan's. "Be careful."

She took point, heading through the empty galley. With weapons up, they cleared the room, along with the empty cabins and labs.

The entire boat was eerily quiet.

She pointed up the stairs to the bridge, and Dec nodded. They moved silently upward, pausing at the door. A quick glance inside, and she saw bodies on the floor.

Fuck. She didn't spot any hostiles. She gave the signal to move.

Dec went in high, Morgan low. It took them seconds to clear the small space. They found Diego tied to his chair, beaten and bleeding, his chin on his chest. He was unconscious.

Marc and his son were huddled together in a corner, gagged and their hands tied. Hale and Coop were sprawled on the floor.

The bridge was a mess. Maps were torn up and in disarray. Blood splattered one window and the control panel.

Dec went straight to check Hale and Coop. Morgan quickly freed Marc and Turner.

"There you go. Take it easy." She moved to Diego, checking his pulse. Strong and steady.

She lifted his head. He was still out, and one eye was swollen.

Then she heard Hale groan. She released a breath, looking back over her shoulder. He was alive. Sitting up and cradling his head. Dec was helping Coop to sit up.

"What happened?" Dec asked.

"Boarded," Coop bit out. "Four of them. They came out of nowhere, like fucking ghosts." Not many people got the drop on Ronin Cooper, and Morgan could tell he wasn't very happy about it.

"Hale and Coop fought really hard," Marc said with a shake of his head. "They took two of the attackers down." He glanced at the blood. "I think one of them was dead."

"They said Dr. Duncan and Jasmin were tied up in their cabins," Hale added.

"We'll find them," Dec said.

"They took Marc and Turner hostage next," Hale said. "So we had to comply. They knocked Coop and me out."

Take the most dangerous hostages out of action. Morgan nodded. It was what she would have done.

"They wanted all the information on the *Soleil d'Orient*," Marc added. "The captain refused to give it to them. They wanted to access the computer and pull data," Marc said with a cold smile. "He told them to go fuck themselves."

"Come on, Torres." Morgan patted the man's face. "Rise and shine."

Diego groaned, and opened one eye. "Fuck. Ward, you'd better give me a good bonus after this."

"Yeah, yeah," Dec said wryly, but Morgan noticed relief in his voice. "What did they get?"

"Paper maps and notes only." Diego groaned again, probing his swollen eye. "No electronic data."

Dec patted his shoulder. "Good man. You shouldn't have risked your life, though."

Diego's reply was a snort. "This is my dive too, now."

Morgan cupped his stubbled jaw. "How's the head feel?"

"My head is throbbing like a son of a bitch." He shot her a smile. "You want to play nurse with me, lovely Morgan?"

She landed a not-very-gentle punch to his shoulder. "I think you're fine."

Dec looked at Morgan. "Hale and I will clear the ship and check on Taye and Jasmin. Coop, you stay here. Morgan, check on Zach and his team, and give them an update. Bring Zach up, along with a first aid kit."

When she came back out on deck, the archeologists were all waiting nervously.

"What's happened?" Zach asked, concerned.

"The ship was boarded by a team. A good team. They were after all your data on the shipwreck."

Zach cursed, and behind him, his team gasped.

"Dec and Hale are clearing the ship," she said.

"But whoever it was, it looks like they've left. For now, everyone wait here." She looked at Zach. "We need you on the bridge."

He nodded. "Okay."

Morgan strode into the galley and pulled out the first aid kit. She saw Zach's eyes widen. "Is someone hurt?"

"They're all a bit battered. Diego copped the worst of it. He refused to give them access to the computer system." She headed back to the bridge, a grim-faced Zach following her.

They met Dec and Hale on the stairs, followed by Taye and Jasmin. Both looked fine, but a little shaken.

"Ship's clear," Dec said.

"Taye, can you round up the others?" Zach asked. "Secure the artifacts and then send everyone off to shower and change."

The archeologist nodded. "Consider it done."

On the bridge, Morgan moved straight to Diego, popped the kit open, and grabbed a quick-cool icepack. She snapped it, and once it was cold, pressed it to his swelling eye.

"Knew you wanted to play nurse with me," Diego drawled.

Morgan ignored him, getting out some antiseptic wipes. Behind her, she heard a sound that was an awful lot like a growl. She glanced back and saw Zach scowling at Diego.

She swiped the blood off Diego's face, then stood and patted him on the head. He groaned. "There's a good patient."

"You have a terrible bedside manner."

She walked over to Zach and Dec.

"The intruders got paper maps and notes, but nothing electronic," Dec said.

Zach blew out a breath, his hands on his hips. "Who would be this brazen? It must be unscrupulous treasure hunters. Thieves."

Morgan shared a look with Dec. "Probably." She hoped that was all it was.

"My team will change our tactics to ensure we don't get surprised again. Coop and Hale managed to take two of the four down. They know we aren't a soft target." A grim smile appeared on Dec's face. "Besides, they won't catch Coop so easily again."

"There is one possibility we should discuss," Morgan said, with a glance at Dec, Coop, and Hale. "Silk Road."

Zach straightened. "Silk Road? The antiquities thieves?"

She nodded. "We've had a few run-ins with them before. This smells like them."

"Is there something on the *Soleil d'Orient* that would interest them?" Dec asked.

"They like fancy artifacts, with long, legendary histories," Morgan said. "Regular treasure might interest them, but it's the truly priceless stuff they usually go after."

"Like the lost treasures of Zerzura, or the Cintamani stone," Zach suggested.

Morgan nodded, memories of those past missions flashing through her head. "Yes, just like that."

"I can't think of anything. You've seen the list of treasures that were on the *Soleil d'Orient*. Unless those Japanese plates have some mystical legend attached to them that I don't know about."

But again, Morgan thought she saw the faintest hint of something cross Zach's face. For a second, she thought he was going to add something else, then he closed his mouth.

Dec nodded. "All right. Go and get cleaned up. I'm sure your team needs some reassurance. Warn them to stay cautious and bring up anything they notice that seems out of the ordinary, or that concerns them."

With a nod, Zach left the bridge. Morgan walked to the window, watching him carefully as he descended the stairs. He was tense, not moving with his usual smooth stride.

The sexy archeologist was worried. That was understandable. But Morgan's gut was telling her the doctor knew more than he was telling them. And she wanted to know what the man was hiding.

Chapter Seven

Zach leaned over the tray that held one of the porcelain vases they'd brought up from the wreck.

He gently cleaned away the soluble salts in fresh water. Next up, he'd have to scrape off the encrusted deposits with scalpels and an ultrasonic chisel. The afternoon dive had gone well, with Taye leading it. They'd found several more vases, and a few other artifacts.

But as thrilling as working on a new artifact was, he couldn't stop thinking about the attack. He was damned grateful that Hale, Coop, and Diego only had minor injuries. What if his students or archeologists had been attacked? What if Morgan had been hurt?

Then his thoughts turned to Silk Road. Air whistled through his teeth as he hissed out a breath. There wasn't a shred of evidence out there that any sort of important artifact was aboard the *Soleil d'Orient*. Sure, he had his own theories and suspicions...

What if Silk Road had pieced together the same fantastic clues he had, and come up with their own theory? Maybe he should just tell Dec and Morgan.

No, it just wasn't possible that Silk Road knew

anything. And Zach would be risking not only his career, but his team's, if unsubstantiated rumors and theories were spread with their names attached to them. He needed evidence and facts, first.

Something made him look up. He saw Morgan leaning against the door frame, watching him.

"When did you come in? I didn't hear you."

She shrugged. "I only make a sound when I want someone to know I'm there. You have a very serious look on your face, Dr. James."

He motioned to the vase in the tray. "Cleaning and caring for artifacts is a serious business."

"What have you discovered?"

"It'll take a while to get the vases clean, but my guess is we have some Chinese porcelain under here." He only had hints of the pattern, but once it was clean, he'd be able to tell more.

"That's promising." She walked toward him, studying him.

He felt like an artifact under heavy scrutiny. "What?"

"Dinner's ready," she said.

He nodded. The vase would wait. He washed his hands, and then followed Morgan to the galley. Everyone was already in there, clustered around the tables and eating. His team looked happy, and he could hear their conversation about the dives.

They'd shaken off the attack pretty easily. He glanced over at the Treasure Hunter Security crew, who looked somber and thoughtful. They had not.

He grabbed a plate and filled it from the food

laid out in trays. Turned out Marc was quite the chef. There was also a tray of beers, and Morgan snagged a bottle and held it out to him.

"Are you having one?" he asked.

She nodded. "Dec and Coop are on watch tonight."

They sat down at an empty table. She nodded toward his team. "They look happy."

He nodded. "Today's discoveries are exciting. Some digs and dives turn up nothing, so to find something so soon is always a thrill." He speared some chicken with his fork. "But we still need to find the main part of the ship."

She took a sip of her beer. "We'll find it." She cocked her head. "I read the list of treasure that was on the ship again. There was a fair bit of detail, except for one line listed as a gift from M. Constance. Who was that?"

"Monsieur Constance. That's what the French called Constantine Phaulkon."

"The mysterious Mr. Phaulkon again. Tell me more about him?"

"Like I said before, he was a Greek adventurer. He ran away at eleven, and got his start as a cabin boy on a ship. He worked his way up to clerk for the British East India Company in Java. He clearly had a knack for languages, and spoke Greek, English, French, Portuguese, Malay, and Thai."

"Smart guy."

"I read a description of him that said 'a fire burned inside him.' He was clearly ambitious, but everything changed when he moved to Siam. He quickly became a favorite of the king, and was given important positions at court. A French ambassador said 'he was one of those in the world who have the most wit, liberality, magnificence, intrepidity, and was full of great projects.' In Siam, he was a charismatic guy who wielded a lot of influence."

"So what was this gift he put on the ship?"

Zach shrugged. "No one knows."

They finished their meal, and Morgan headed over to the tray of desserts. She came back with a plate loaded high with anything and everything chocolate, topped by chocolate syrup.

He winced as he thought of the sugar content. "How the hell do you stay in shape if you eat chocolate in that quantity?"

She took a bite of cake, chewed, swallowed. "Good metabolism." She took another bite and made a small humming noise of pleasure.

That noise went straight to Zach's cock, making it twitch. *Damn*. He shifted in his seat to relieve the pressure.

For him, being with a woman was always fun. Good times, with no commitments. Easy, and over. He was dedicated to his work, and he'd come from parents who were extremely inept at relationships, so he knew that anything long-term just wasn't for him.

Morgan, on the other hand... He knew there was nothing easy about her, but she made him think about things he'd never thought of before. He hadn't had her in his bed, hadn't even kissed her properly, but he thought about things like waking up curled around her, listening to her laugh, and watching her eat chocolate with obvious enjoyment.

Maybe he was coming down with something.

Finally, she sat back, her plate empty except for a tell-tale smear of syrup. "Diego had his guys bring a foosball table out on deck. Want to play?"

"Sure." Zach stood, snagging his bottle of beer. Morgan was being nice to him, and that made him nervous. He preferred it when he felt the sharp edge of her teeth.

When they headed out onto the deck, the evening had cooled off, but it was still pleasant. The sun was long gone, the moon high in the night sky, and with the lights on the ship, the deck was illuminated. They made their way over to a battered foosball table.

"I have to warn you, I'm pretty good at this." Her teeth flashed in the darkness.

"Let's see what you've got, Kincaid."

As they played, she muttered under her breath, her hands moving over the controls. She was beautiful in the moonlight, which was a distraction, and she was also ultracompetitive.

When she won the game, she threw her hands in the air. "I win!"

"I should've guessed you'd be cutthroat."

"I completed BUD/S training. That should have warned you."

"True."

"Best of three?" she asked.

He tilted his head. "And if I win? What do I get?"

She watched him steadily. "What do you want?"

"A kiss." The words were out of him before he realized. They stared at each other.

After a minute that hummed between them, she nodded. "Okay, Dr. James. You're on."

Her words were a jolt to his system. His gaze dropped to her lips. "And if you win?"

She smiled and it was sharp. Warning bells rang in his head.

"You tell me what you think Constantine Phaulkon put on the *Soleil d'Orient.*"

***

Zach frowned. "I don't know what you—"

"Don't lie to me." Morgan's tone was sharper than she'd intended. "Flirt. Banter all you want. But don't lie to me."

His smile dissolved, his face turning serious. "Okay."

"So you do suspect he put more than gold on the ship."

"Maybe. But there is no way Silk Road could know that. It can't be them after the wreck."

He didn't know Silk Road like she did. She focused her attention on the table, and they played.

Morgan pressed her hip against the table, moving her fingers fast, jerking her players to kick the ball. When Zach won the game, she fought back a scowl. "You're competitive, too."

"When you grow up with nothing, you learn to fight for what you want."

There was a dark edge to his voice that didn't jive with the Zach James she knew. "Rough childhood?"

"Takes one to know one."

"I had a great childhood. Sure, my mom died, but my dad was awesome." She wrinkled her nose. "My teens may have been a little rough, having a father who was completely perplexed by his little girl growing into a woman. But it wasn't bad." Until he was ripped away from her in the most horrible way.

"Well, there was nothing great about mine." He shrugged. "Let's just say I like winning."

"So do I."

They started the third and final game. They played hard, and Morgan found herself ramming her hip against the table with each move. Zach's focus was laser-sharp. Morgan didn't take her gaze off the players, and felt a trickle of sweat down her spine. She *had* to win. She *always* won.

The ball flew into the goal.

Zach had won.

Shit. Morgan stepped back. She never lost at foosball.

She looked over at him, expecting to see one of those sexy grins of his spread across his face. Instead, his green eyes were intense, his expression stark.

He circled the table with intent and she felt herself stiffen.

"I still want to know what you aren't telling me."

He stopped an inch from her. "You tell me a

secret about you, and I'll tell you one about me."

She lifted one shoulder. "Some secrets are best left in the dark."

He pinned her against the table. The two of them were completely alone, the only sounds their quiet breathing and the gentle lap of water against the hull of the boat.

"I'll be careful with your secrets, Morgan," he said quietly.

She lifted her chin. "You? Mr. Adventuring Archeologist?"

Zach cupped her chin. "I know when something needs taking care of."

A frisson of heat ran through her, but she managed a snort. "I'm not delicate."

His finger stroked against her jawline, the touch making goose bumps break out on her skin. "Maybe not this tough, sexy exterior, but what about what's beneath it?"

Morgan couldn't take all this gentle wooing. She wanted hard, rough heat. She wrapped her hands around his biceps, and yanked him closer, so that her breasts pressed hard against his chest. "Don't worry about what's on the inside. This is about physical attraction, Dr. James, that's it."

He wrapped his arms around her. "Oh?"

"It's about desire." Sure, mind-blowing, panty-melting desire, but that was all this was. A chemical reaction.

"Just sex?" he murmured.

"Hold your horses, Casanova. The bet was for one kiss. I didn't say anything about sex."

He lowered his head until his lips were a whisper away from hers. "One kiss."

Then his mouth touched hers.

She parted her lips and his tongue entered, slicking over hers. She moaned, tangling her tongue with his. He tasted like beer and sex. Pulling him closer, she deepened the kiss. She wanted more.

He was so warm and she suddenly realized how cold she was.

He made a low sound in his throat, his hands sliding down to cup her ass. He pulled her closer, and she felt the hard bulge in the front of his shorts.

Morgan slid her hands up into his shaggy hair. The kiss turned rough, addictive. She'd never had a kiss send her up in flames like this. It felt endless, and it also felt like it would never be enough.

The sound of voices not too far away made them jerk away from each other. Morgan murmured a curse. She felt rattled, her legs unsteady. She wished she could blame it on the rolling waves beneath the ship, but she knew that would be a lie.

"Christ," Zach muttered.

"Time to call it a night." If her words tumbled out too quickly, she hoped he didn't notice. "We've got a big day of diving tomorrow."

Zach ran a hand through his hair. "Right. Diving. Yeah, sure."

She smiled to herself. He was just as rattled as she was. That helped soothe some of her nerves. "I'll see you in the morning, Dr. James."

"Count on it." But he just stood there, staring at her. "I want you, Morgan. And I'm going to have you."

Her pulse spiked. "I'm not a prize for you to win, and I have a say in this too."

"You want me."

Damn. She couldn't deny that. "Good night."

For a second, he looked like he was going to reach out and grab her. But then he stepped back and she felt a stab of disappointment mixed with relief.

"Sleep well, Morgan."

Morgan stayed where she was, pressed against the foosball table, and watched him walk away.

She blew out a breath. Sleep well. *Yeah, right.* She was pretty sure she knew what—or rather whom—would star in her dreams tonight.

Chapter Eight

Zach splashed water on his face, and looked at himself in the mirror above the tiny sink in his cabin.

He needed to shave, but he usually left the scruff when he was out in the field. He'd slept, but not very well. He'd had dreams, so many dreams. So many good dreams.

Trying not to think about long, toned legs wrapped around his waist, or Morgan's mouth traveling over his skin, he headed to the galley. It was empty, and he took a second to grab a slice of toast and a boiled egg.

After eating and tossing back a quick coffee, he headed out onto the deck.

The first thing he saw was Morgan.

The taste and feel of her slammed into him, memories peppering him like bullets. Today, he had a full day of diving, looking for a wreck that he'd dreamed about for a very long time, but for the first time in his life, he was just as excited about spending the day with this woman.

"You look like a starving man who just spotted a juicy steak."

Hale's voice made Zach wrench his gaze off

Morgan. The big man was wearing dark cargo shorts and a white polo shirt that contrasted with his skin.

"Pretty sure Morgan wouldn't like hearing herself described as a steak."

Hale grinned. "That's the truth. And let me tell you, the woman can land a mean right hook." Then the man's smile faded. "I see the way you watch her and I feel like I should warn you...Morgan has a lot of first dates and not many second ones. She rarely gives a guy much of a chance, and to be fair, none of the ones I've seen her with were worthy of her."

Zach felt his muscles tighten. "You warning me off?"

"If I did that, she'd try and hit me. Morgan is one of the best women I know. In a firefight, I'd have her at my back in a second. But, she guards herself pretty hard, and it would take a determined man to get through."

Zach glanced back at her as she moved in the morning light. "I'm determined. And pretty sneaky." He met Hale's dark eyes. "And I see through the toughness she uses like a shield."

Hale considered him a second, then nodded. "I think you'll do, Dr. James. Oh, and if you hurt her, I'll break every bone in your body."

Zach swallowed. Great, overprotective Navy SEAL alert. "Noted."

"And this conversation never happened."

Zach cocked his head. "Or she'll break your bones too?"

Hale's smile widened. "Yeah, you'll do, doc."

"Got it." Zach made his way across the deck. "Morning."

"Morning." Morgan eyed him. "You're not going to act weird, are you?"

He kept his voice low. "Because I had my tongue in your mouth?"

She raised a brow. "And your hands on my ass."

He grinned at her. God, she was something. "And you were moaning."

Her brows drew together. "No, I wasn't."

"Yes, you were."

"No, I—"

"What are you two arguing about now?" Declan's deep voice came from behind Zach.

"Nothing," Morgan said quickly, shooting Zach a warning glare. She turned and started pulling her wet suit on. "We're just getting ready to get in the water."

Smiling to himself, and feeling pretty darn good, Zach pulled his own wet suit on. The gear and tanks were all laid out for his team. Morgan was very good at double-checking it all and getting it ready.

Nearby, an already-suited-up Declan was getting the airlift pump started. The airlift was a sand suction dredge they could use to suck sand away. It was vacuumed up a pipe, and the debris collected. His students would get the lucky job of examining the collected sand for any small artifacts.

Before long, everyone was tipping over the edge into the water. He watched as Morgan somersaulted back and sank beneath the waves, her fins rising up above the surface to kick as she descended.

Zach followed her in.

Soon, they were all following their dive plan. His team started their searches, swimming backward and forward in regular search patterns. Max had the camera today, and was busy capturing the locations anytime anyone thought they'd found something.

Alice waved Zach over, pointing at the sand. Zach swam down. She'd found what looked like a coin buried in the sand. Carefully, Zach brushed off the sand and pulled the coin out, resting it on his gloved palm. It was worn, and he couldn't see any identifying marks. They'd have to take a more thorough look in the lab. He dropped it gently into his mesh bag.

He hung in the water, watching his team work. They were doing a great job—careful and methodical. His archeologists were taking the time to teach the students.

But a wave of frustration flared. There was still nothing to point them in the direction of the main body of the ship, and nothing that conclusively proved this was the ship they were after.

Minutes passed, and then Jasmin waved him over. Zach floated beside the woman and noticed Morgan swim up beside him. Jasmin pointed down.

There was something buried in the sand.

Working carefully, they dusted the sand off. He waved at Declan, who brought the suction dredge tube over. Declan set the pipe down and vacuumed the sand away from the artifact.

It was a plate. Completely intact.

It was difficult to tell much about it, but it looked like heavily tarnished metal. His pulse spiked. He gestured for Jasmin to pack it up in one of the bags.

Zach looked around. They were finding a good number of small artifacts, but where the hell was the ship, itself? Sure, they weren't going to find a hulking wreck. The *Soleil d'Orient* had been made of wood, so he was looking for rotted wooden planks and more cannons as evidence of the ship's structure.

Soon, Morgan tapped her dive watch. It was time to head up.

Back on the *Storm Nymph*, they all shed their dive gear.

"Let's get the artifacts into the lab," Zach called out, shaking the water out of his hair. "I want to check out that plate."

He wasn't surprised to find everyone packed into the wet lab as he started cleaning the plate. Even the THS team was lined up against the far wall, watching and waiting. There was an air of excitement in the room. Zach carefully swiped his cloth over the plate.

He stared at it. *Oh, God.* "It's made of gold."

He yanked his tablet over, and tapped into one of his research folders. He pulled up the image he wanted, and turned the tablet around. "Look."

There was an old sketch of a golden plate,

similar in size to the one in front of him.

"It's a plate from Japan," he said.

"Japan?" Morgan said. "Like the plates gifted to the King of Siam from the Japanese Emperor?"

Zach lifted the plate, turning it over. He grinned. "I can read the stamp on the back. These plates were made for Emperor Reigen of Japan. He ruled at the same time King Narai ruled Siam. And in turn, Narai gifted the plates to Louis XIV."

Morgan smiled. "The King of Siam was a re-gifter. Cheap." Her smile widened. "But congratulations, Dr. James. Looks like you just found the *Soleil d'Orient*."

Shouts and whoops filled the room.

***

Morgan leaned against the railing, the cool, night air brushing over her shoulders. Behind her, on the deck, the archeologists were celebrating. A few of the students had already had one too many beers. They'd feel it tomorrow when they dived.

She stared down at the dark water and thought of the poor people who'd drowned here. She could imagine the *Soleil d'Orient* pitching in the stormy waves, rain pelting the deck. Panicked shouts and people running in terror.

Now, she looked up in the direction of the shore, and spotted the faint twinkle of lights at Tolagnaro. They'd been so close and yet so far away.

"Hey." Zach leaned on the rail beside her.

He was dangling a beer between his hands. "Dr. James."

"Come on. You *still* won't call me Zach?" He waggled his eyebrows. "We've kissed, so you should at least call me Zach."

"Nope."

"Stubborn. No beer tonight?"

She shook her head. "I'm on watch this evening. But you certainly have something to celebrate."

"It's here." A flash of his white teeth. "History. It's right here beneath the waves."

"Time to tell me what else you think might be down there," she said.

He sipped his beer. "I told you, I'll share mine when you share something about yourself."

She looked out at the water. She wasn't a talker. Talking about herself and her feelings never made her feel better. There were a lot of things she'd never shared with anyone. Even her friends at THS.

But something about easygoing Zachariah James made her want to talk. "I was sixteen when my dad was killed." The pain was a bright slash on her heart.

"Sorry about your dad. What happened?"

"A random, senseless murder. He was gunned down on the street during a robbery. They never caught the guy. I didn't want to go into foster care. In fact, I was terrified of it. I ran away."

"And went where?"

She sucked in a breath. "I lived on the streets until I turned eighteen and joined the Navy."

She felt him staring at her, and it made her skin itch.

Morgan glanced his way, and the look on his face made her stiffen. "Don't you dare look at me with pity—"

"I'm not." He grabbed her arm. "I'm looking at you with admiration. That couldn't have been safe. A young girl alone on the streets."

"That's where I learned how to defend myself." She tried to smile, but dark memories pushed at her. Things she didn't want to think about, when she'd been terrifyingly alone.

He reached out and traced the scar on her cheek.

She cleared her throat. "A man attacked me while I was sleeping. I survived and he regretted the decision."

Something hot burned in Zach's eyes. "Hence the admiration."

"So, I shared, and now it's your turn."

She saw his fingers tighten on the beer bottle. "What do you want to know?"

She was curious as to whatever he was being cagey about in regard to the wreck, but now she also really wanted to know more about the man. "Tell me about this rough childhood."

"It's not a pretty story." He took another long pull of his beer. "I grew up in a trailer park. My mom ran off before I could even remember her, and my dad was a bad-tempered drunk."

Simple words hiding a wealth of pain.

"I was the nerdy, scrawny kid that everyone picked on at school."

She eyed him up and down, taking in his muscular form. "No way."

"Yep." A faint smile. "But I didn't care about what anyone said, not when I was busy dodging my father's rages. Books were my escape. I devoured history books about Egypt, Greece, Rome, China, shipwrecks, anything I could get my hands on. They helped me stay sane."

Morgan's heart clenched for the young boy he'd been. "So what happened to that geeky, scrawny kid?"

"He finished high school and managed to get a scholarship to college. I escaped. I left that trailer and I never looked back."

Much as she'd done after she lost her dad. She'd found the Navy, and he'd found history.

"I decided to work on preserving that history I'd read about in those books. I wanted to uncover it and share it with others. I wanted to make something of myself, and have as many adventures as I could pack into my life."

He was still running from that trailer park, she realized. And what he'd suffered in it.

"Night, Dr. James." Charity's bubbly voice broke through the evening. "Night, Morgan."

"We're off to bed," Jasmin called out.

Behind them, the tipsy students were heading to their bunks. Zach raised a hand. "I guess everyone's calling it a night. We do have an early start tomorrow."

"And I need to do a round of the ship." Dec was being extra vigilant, to ensure they didn't get any more uninvited visitors.

They stared at each other for a long moment, the air heating.

He reached out, his fingers brushing the shell of her ear. "Goodnight, Morgan."

How could one simple touch leave her heart beating so hard? "Goodnight, Dr. James."

He walked across the deck, and joined his team, his easy laugh drifting across the deck. He might still be running from his past, but he'd made something good of his life. He hadn't let it scar him.

Morgan looked back at the dark waves. She wasn't sure she could say the same. She had a good job, friends, but she knew something else was missing.

She wanted more, but she was well-aware that she didn't like letting people close. And the few times she'd tried, they hadn't wanted to stick around.

But, damn. A certain sexy, charming archeologist was slowly but steadily working his way under her skin.

Chapter Nine

He was dreaming of Morgan.

Zach groaned. In his dream, Morgan rolled on top of him, her strong legs squeezing his hips. She leaned down, her mouth taking his in a hard, hungry kiss. She nipped his bottom lip, and he tasted the copper flavor of blood. It was so good. He groaned again.

Then her hands moved up, over his chest, to his neck. They circled his throat...

And squeezed tight.

Choking, he started coughing. Suddenly, the image of Morgan was gone, and he just saw a dark shadow.

He couldn't breathe. He jerked awake, struggling to sit up.

There was a wire at his throat, digging in hard. He choked, feeling his lungs starting to burn. He grabbed at the wire, trying to get his fingers beneath it.

It was jerked back harder, his neck stinging. Lack of air was making him dizzy.

"Tell me the exact location of the ship." The voice at his ear was low, whispered. He couldn't even tell if it was a man or a woman.

Zach shook his head. "Don't...know," he gasped out.

"Tell me where to find the amulet."

Oh, no. "What...amulet?"

He was jerked back again. Hard. "Don't make this harder than it has to be."

Screw this. Zach jammed his elbow back. It hit flesh, and his attacker groaned. Zach slammed his body sideways, tossing himself and his attacker off the narrow bunk. They thudded into the desk, then fell to the floor. The wire around Zach's neck loosened, and he drew in a deep breath. In the next second, his attacker landed on his back, and he fell facedown.

Their combined grunts and muttered curses filled the cabin, and Zach felt the bastard trying to tighten the wire again. Zach thrust his head back, and it smacked against the guy's nose.

With a low curse, his attacker shoved Zach forward. His forehead hit the floor, causing him to see stars. In those few seconds, the bastard tightened the wire, harder than before. With the thin strand of metal digging into his neck, he felt blood sliding down his throat. He struggled for air.

Fuck. He didn't want to die.

Suddenly, the door to his cabin slammed open. "Zach!" Morgan's long silhouette filled the doorway and light spilled inside.

Zach's attacker released him and launched forward. All he saw was a dark shadow hitting her knees, sending her stumbling. Then the attacker was gone, racing down the corridor.

Nausea rose in Zach's throat, dizziness threatening to take over. He pushed up on all fours, but that was as far as he could go. He touched his throat. It was sticky with blood. As he sucked in air, his breathing was a harsh, forced sound.

With a curse, Morgan appeared by his side, crouching next to him. The light flicked on in the cabin, and he blinked. Her hands went to his neck, pushing his away.

"Let me take a look." Her touch was gentle. "Shit." She was wearing a loose shirt over her tank top, and she pulled it off. She wadded up the material, and pressed it against his neck. "God, Zach." Her voice trembled.

His gaze sharpened on her, vision clearing. There was a storm of emotion on her face. She looked like she was about to lose it.

A jumble of voices rumbled in the corridor.

"What the hell's going on?"

"My God, Zach."

Morgan raised her voice. "Somebody get the first aid kit." Her words rang with authority. "And someone find Declan."

Zach heard people moving and talking, but he didn't pay any attention. He worked on not emptying his stomach on the floor.

"The rest of you get back to your cabins," Morgan said. "Stay there until someone from my team comes to talk to you. Don't open the door to a stranger."

Zach liked listening to Morgan's voice, even when it held an edge. His vision blurred again. He was really afraid he was going to pass out.

"Come on, Zach." Cool fingers touched his face. "Look at me."

He did, staring into her aqua-blue eyes. His chest loosened a little. "I finally got you to call me Zach."

Her fingers stroked his cheek and she rolled her eyes. "That's really all you can think about right now?"

"Yes. Apparently, all I needed was for someone to choke me half to death."

Her face darkened. "Don't joke about it."

"Help me up. I'd prefer to not be sitting on my ass when Declan arrives."

She slid an arm around his shoulders, and helped him sit on the edge of his bunk. Moments later, Declan arrived, first aid kit in hand.

"What happened?" he demanded.

"Someone attacked Zach." Morgan lifted her shirt off his neck.

Declan winced and then muttered a creative curse.

"They attacked me in my sleep," he told them. "They were demanding to know the exact location of the shipwreck."

Declan crossed his arms over his chest, watching as Morgan started cleaning Zach's wound. "No one got aboard. We've tightened up the patrols day and night. Morgan, you see any sign that someone came aboard the ship?"

She shook her head.

"I've got Coop and Hale looking around," Declan

added. "I am getting tired of feeling two steps behind."

Morgan passed a wipe across Zach's wound. "It's not too bad." She let out a shaky breath.

"It feels bad," he complained. "Maybe you should kiss it better?"

She snorted. "Keep dreaming." But despite her words, he felt her fingers gently brushing the back of his neck.

"Anything else you can tell us?" Declan asked. "What they looked like?"

Zach shook his head. "No. They stayed behind me and whispered. They were smaller than me, dressed in black. Couldn't even tell if it was a man or a woman."

"They were wearing a balaclava," Morgan added. "And once I find them, they're dead."

Morgan's deadly tone made Zach freeze.

Declan drew in a long breath. "Stand down, Morgan."

"They were trying to *kill* him, Dec." Anger sizzled in her tone.

Zach reached up, grabbed her hand and squeezed. Her aqua eyes met his, then she dropped her gaze and rubbed something on his neck. He hissed at the sting. "They also asked about an amulet."

Morgan's hands stilled. Her gaze came back to his face. "An amulet? What amulet?"

"I'm not sure. There was no specific jewelry on the ship's manifest—"

"That's not an answer," she said. "This is what

you've been keeping to yourself, isn't it?"

"It's a legend," Zach bit out. "Nothing else. There's no proof that some pendant with a magical power existed, let alone that it was on the *Soleil d'Orient.*"

A muscle ticked in Declan's jaw. "What amulet?"

Morgan's gaze narrowed. "Magical power?"

Zach lifted his chin. "I'm an archeologist. I deal in fact. I deal in the artifacts and evidence I dig out of the ground or rescue from the sea."

Declan nodded. "Fine. Then I think it's time you talked to us about myths and legends." His gray gaze moved to Morgan. "Clean up the wound, and then both of you meet me in the galley. I'm going to check in with the archeologists and students."

Morgan finished with his neck, pressing a bandage over the long wound. She snapped the lid of the first aid box closed.

"Morgan—"

"I asked you if there was anything that might interest Silk Road."

"There *isn't.* There is no record this amulet ever existed, let alone that it was on the ship. If I truly believed it was there, I would have said something." He shook his head. "Without something concrete in your hand, you have nothing." He knew that better than anyone. A hard truth he'd learned growing up.

"They almost killed you!" The words burst out of her. "You would have died right here. A bloody, senseless murder."

Silence filled the cabin. A bloody, senseless

murder...like what had happened to her father. "Morgan—"

With a violent shake of her head, she shot to her feet. "Come on, we need to get to the galley."

Zach didn't push her, but he felt the tension pumping off her as they headed out of his cabin. The galley was all lit up, the THS team sitting around a table with Diego. Feeling very tired, Zach dropped into a chair.

"We've searched the ship and there is no sign of your attacker," Declan said. "No sign anyone came aboard. If I'm going to work out what the hell is going on, I need something to work with."

Moments later, Morgan brought Zach a coffee. He smiled his thanks, and he curled his hands around the mug. It had a chip on the edge, and he worried it with his finger. "Shit, where do I start?" His voice was raw, and he carefully cleared his throat.

"At the beginning," Declan suggested.

"I told you about Constantine Phaulkon, and his meteoric rise to power in Siam. He influenced everyone around him. Whatever he said, people listened, agreed, and believed. Before he reached Siam, he worked for the British East India Company in Java."

He looked up, and saw them all watching him steadily.

"Go on," Declan said.

"One of my specialties is underwater archeology, but I have another."

"Prehistoric cultures," Morgan said.

"So, the really old stuff," Declan added.

Zach nodded. "My research over the last year has focused on submerged megalithic structures."

"Sunken cities?" Hale asked.

"Yes."

Now Declan's eyebrows rose. "Atlantis."

"No." Zach looked at all of them. "The legends and stories about Atlantis are mostly exaggerated, bogus crap. But the sunken structures I've dived are real."

"A seed of truth is in every myth," Declan murmured. "That's what Layne is always telling me."

Zach nodded. "It's possible the Atlantis myths are a remembrance of something else, long ago."

"Civilization before what current history tells us?" Morgan said.

"Perhaps. But I meant what I said earlier. I deal in facts and proof." He took a sip of the coffee, letting it warm him. "For an archeologist to throw out unsubstantiated theories is a death blow for your career. My colleagues are not quick to embrace anything untested."

"But you believe advanced cultures existed before the last Ice Age," Morgan prompted. "And were wiped out by a flood."

"Wiped out by rapidly rising sea levels at the end of the Ice Age. I've already told Morgan, but last year I dived what looked like a man-made structure off the southern coast of India. It is possibly nine thousand years old."

"That's far older than Egypt," Declan said.

"And Sumer," Hale added.

"There are other alleged sunken cities off the coast of India. Tamil literature in southern India is rife with legends of Kumari Kundan."

"Which is what?" Morgan asked.

"A lost continent in the Indian Ocean that was destroyed by the waves. It was said to have stretched from Indonesia up to India, and down to...Madagascar."

"Hell," Hale said. "There would be geological evidence of something like that."

"There is. Many scientists believe that there were at least land bridges linking Madagascar up with India. Not everyone agrees on how large those bridges were, but there was likely land in the Indian Ocean thousands of years ago."

Coop cleared his throat. "I've heard of a lost continent in the Indian Ocean. Lemuria."

Zach nodded. "Named after Madagascar's famous lemurs. A zoologist in the 1800s coined the name of a lost continent in the Indian Ocean. He'd discovered lemur fossils in Madagascar and India, and proposed they'd once been part of a continent that is now submerged. This was before the theory of continental drift. Madagascar split away from Africa first, then India, which would also account for the fossils."

"So, no Lemuria, but possibly some land bridges," Morgan said.

"Madagascar was settled by a group of Indonesians, likely over two thousand years ago. The belief is they managed to cross the ocean to get here, then over time mixed with African settlers to give us the Malagasy of today. But back to Lemuria, there is no scientific evidence, and what stories exist are too polluted by New Age-mystical beliefs to gain any facts from them, but—"

"There's a seed of truth," Morgan finished.

Again, Zach nodded.

"Okay, that is all fascinating stuff, but how does this link to Phaulkon and the *Soleil d'Orient?*" Morgan asked.

"In Indonesia, there is evidence of a sunken continent known as Sundaland. Strangely enough, the original location of the Madagascan settlers. While Phaulkon was stationed in Java, he visited Gunung Padang."

Morgan frowned. "Which is what?"

Declan sat back in his chair. "It's a pyramid."

Coop leaned forward, his brow furrowed. "Pyramids in Indonesia?"

Zach nodded. "Yes. There is still a lot of argument about whether it's natural or man-made. But there is evidence of megalithic structures built on the mound."

"So, Phaulkon visited it," Declan prompted.

"Yes. And from a letter he sent back home to Greece, he found something there. He mentioned an amulet." Zach pulled out his tablet. "This is a well-known portrait of Constantine Phaulkon." He held the tablet out so they could all see the image. Zach pointed to the pendant around the man's neck. "This shows a pendant that he apparently rarely took off. Within a year of finding this artifact, he went from a nobody merchant for the British East India Company to the highest advisor of the King of Siam."

Chapter Ten

Morgan paced the deck, a tight ball of emotion centered in her chest.

She pulled her knife out of its sheath on her belt, flicking the hilt around her hand. She was pissed. At everything and everyone.

But most of all, she wanted to find out who the hell had attacked Zach.

She sucked in a long breath of sea air. The image of seeing him down on the floor, a garrote wire digging into his throat, wouldn't fade in a hurry. When the attacker had rammed into her, she'd been so tempted to follow.

But she'd had to make sure Zach was okay. Seeing him on his hands and knees, struggling to breathe and bleeding had terrified her.

Shit. She shook her head. She'd been doing a patrol of the ship, when she'd heard the faintest sound coming from the cabins. She'd almost talked herself out of checking, worried about running into him all rumpled from sleep.

If she hadn't gone down there...

Quiet footsteps behind her. "Morgan?"

Now the angry emotions in her changed target.

She spun and speared him with a look. "Go to bed, Dr. James."

"You called me Zach before." He stood with his hands in his pockets. "You can't take it back now."

"Fine. Go to bed, Zach."

"You're angry with me. I get it. I'm sorry I didn't mention the amulet sooner. But look, I don't even think it's real."

She crossed her arms over her chest, ensuring her knife was in full view.

He glanced at the blade and ignored it. "Even if it does exist, it's just a piece of jewelry. It doesn't have magical powers of persuasion."

"Silk Road must believe it. They don't just go after any old artifact. They must believe it has value."

"We don't even know if it is Silk Road who's involved."

Her mouth tightened. She knew it was Silk Road. It had the group's dirty fingerprints all over it. "You don't think this amulet has some sort of powers?"

He shook his head. "No. Of course not."

That made her smile. "You don't believe in magic, Zach?"

"No. But…"

As his voice trailed off, she turned away from the railing, her brows drawing together. "But what?"

"I do believe that it's possible that these cultures wiped out by rising sea levels may have had advanced technology we don't know about."

Hell. "You can't be serious."

"It's just a theory."

"What kind of tech?"

He huffed out a breath, setting his hands on his hips. "Again. It's just theories. Have you heard of the Baghdad Battery?"

She nodded. "Some artifact that some people theorize was an ancient battery."

"It's Mesopotamian. No one knows what it was, and no one has proved that it was actually a battery. But there are lots of out-of-place artifacts that spawn lots of theories of possible advanced technology from long-ago cultures. The Antikythera Mechanism, the Quimbaya artifacts, the Dendera light, just to name a few. And there are lots of myths, from Egypt to Tibet, about so-called vibration technology that could levitate large stones and carve out tunnels."

Now Morgan slumped back against the rail. "On this job, I've seen everything from shards of pots to golden statues dug up out of the earth. I've seen a giant jewel said to grant wishes and an Amazonian salve that can heal wounds in minutes, but I've never seen anything like what you're talking about."

"I haven't, either. But sometimes I wonder if the broken fragments and shards we dig up are remnants of something we don't understand. Imagine if there was a catastrophe today, and people of the future were digging up our technology. Shattered electronics would give no clue to what a computer was capable of. What would those people think they were?"

Morgan ran a hand over her hair. Hell, he had a point.

"If the amulet does exist," Zach said, "there's a chance it has some sort of tech in it. But look, it's unlikely. Possible, but unlikely."

She watched the way the moonlight cast shadows across his handsome face. "Any other secrets you're hiding, Doc?"

He stepped closer, trapping her against the railing. She felt the warmth pouring off his hard body.

"No. I'm thirty-five years old, employed, and single. I own a two-bedroom condo in downtown Denver. It's in a nice building, but my decorating is pretty sad—white walls, no art, and not much furniture. I haven't had a long-term relationship in...well, ever. I'm too busy with my work, which I love. I also love to travel, be out on field digs and dives. I love history and adventure. I'm not closed-minded, I will look at any and all theories, but I want proof. Oh, and I'm insanely attracted to a deadly, stubborn, fascinating woman."

She stared at him, unable to find any words. She was starting to realize that Zachariah James wasn't just the carefree, Indiana Jones-type she'd pegged him to be. He was far more dangerous.

"You were hurt," she said, her voice hitching. "You should get some sleep. I have a few more hours of work left, yet."

"Morgan, if you want to know anything about me, you just have to ask." He held his arms out to the sides. "For you, I'm an open book."

A reluctant smile tugged at her lips. "I'll keep that in mind."

He reached out, touching her hair. "Stay safe out here."

She lifted her knife and then pointed to her holstered SIG.

He nodded. "Have I told you how sexy I find it that you're armed?"

She shook her head with a smile. "Go to bed, or you might end up with another wound."

He gave her a sloppy salute that made her wince, then slipped down the stairs to the cabins.

Her smile faded. Who had attacked him? It was time to find out what the hell had happened here tonight.

Morgan finished another patrol of the deck, searching for any sign that someone had climbed aboard the *Storm Nymph*. Nothing. She passed the arm of the crane and the storage rack holding all the dive gear. Then she heard the faintest scuff of sound.

Her muscles tensed and she lifted her knife, gripping the hilt. When she heard a sound from the deeper shadows beside the dive gear rack, she spun and tossed the knife.

There was a faint curse. One she recognized.

She let out a breath and straightened. "Really bad idea to sneak up on me, Coop."

Ronin came out of the shadows, eyeing the knife still stuck into the metal. "So you thought you'd throw a knife, first?"

"I'm a bit twitchy." And burning with the need to find out who the hell had tried to kill Zach.

"It nearly hit me."

Footsteps sounded, and a second later, Dec appeared, Hale right behind him. "We searched the entire ship. No sign that anyone came aboard."

Morgan frowned looking around. "We would've seen them."

Dec nodded. "So…"

"So, it looks like it was someone who is already on board." Damn, she didn't like this.

The men all muttered curses.

"Zach said he thought his attacker was smaller than him," Morgan said.

"That rules out Diego and his crew," Dec added. "And I trust Diego with my life."

Morgan nodded. Diego was a part of the Treasure Hunter Security family, even if he wasn't on the permanent payroll. "So that leaves Zach's team."

Dec nodded unhappily. "We keep our eyes and ears open. This amulet changes everything. Even if it doesn't exist, I think Silk Road believes it does." Dec rubbed the back of his neck. "I'll have Darcy start digging into the background of all the archeological team. Apart from Zach, we can't trust any of them."

"Let's hope we have no more excitement tonight," Hale said.

Morgan looked at Hale. "My watch shift is finished. You ready to take over?"

The big man nodded. "Get some sleep."

Morgan headed down to the cabins, and despite a fierce mental argument with herself, she stopped in front of Zach's door. She'd just check on him. That was all.

Quietly, she picked the lock and entered. She closed the door behind her, and moved toward the bunk. He was sprawled on his back, his chest was bare, and the sheets were tangled around his waist. He'd obviously fallen asleep reading his tablet, because it was still clutched in his hand.

She knelt down beside the bed, and gently moved the tablet away. In the darkness, she could make out the stark whiteness of the bandage across his neck.

God, that fallen-angel face of his was so handsome. In sleep, he even looked boyish. Unable to stop herself, she reached out and brushed his hair back off his forehead. He didn't wake, but he turned his face slightly, pushing into her touch. No one had ever looked at her like this man did. With respect edged with awe that left her breathless.

She'd almost lost him before she even had him.

She pulled her hand away, and then moved to sit with her back against the cabin door. She closed her eyes.

No one was hurting him again.

***

The next morning, Zach's neck was a bit sore, but he was ready to work.

He strode into the galley and saw that his

students and archeologists were already there. They surrounded him, fussing.

Charity touched his bandage. "That must have really hurt."

"You okay, Dr. James?" Max asked, his face concerned. "I...I just can't believe what happened."

"I'm fine." He made a shooing motion with his hand. "Go. Finish eating."

Once they'd all resumed their seats again, he filled a bowl with cereal and milk, and sat down with Alice.

"I don't like this, Zach," the archeologist said. "People attacking the ship. You getting hurt."

Zach didn't like it much, either. "The THS guys are here, and they are being more careful than ever. We're in good hands."

Alice shook her head. "The sooner we find the main part of the *Soleil d'Orient* and bring up any artifacts, the better."

"I agree, Alice." Zach spooned some cereal and casually looked around.

"Looking for someone?" she asked with a grin.

"No, I—"

"You're a terrible liar, Zach. I believe our leggy and frankly scary female security agent is out getting the dive gear ready. She said something about checking it three times to ensure nothing's been tampered with."

Zach made a non-committal noise.

Alice shook her head. "Like I said, a terrible liar."

Zach ignored his friend and finished his

breakfast. Soon, he was out on deck. He stared up at the cloudless blue sky. It was a beautiful day for diving.

Ahead, Morgan was already in her wet suit, laying out dive gear. As he approached, she looked up, eyeing his neck. He'd left the bandage off.

"Feel okay?"

He nodded. "Stings a bit, but I'm fine." He started pulling his wet suit on.

"Good." Her voice was a little clipped, and she turned back to the dive gear.

He frowned. He was learning to read Morgan pretty well. "You're angry—"

"You're observant." She lifted the tanks and gestured for him to turn around.

He did, settling his shoulders into the gear and strapping it on. "Morgan, tell me what's—?"

She moved fast, pressing her face close to his. "I hate seeing that injury. It pisses me off."

"I'm okay."

"It's my job to ensure you stay safe."

He cocked his head. "Just your job?" He could smell her. No fancy perfumes for Morgan, just the fresh scent of clean skin.

Her gaze dropped to his lips, then she shoved his fins and mask at him. "Is that everything you need?"

"Yes."

"Good." She shoved him in the chest. Hard. He tipped over the side of the ship and landed in the water with a splash.

Zach came up spluttering, wiping water out of

his eyes. *Goddammit.*

He looked up and saw her smirking at him. Everyone else was calling out with hoots and hollers. He waved them all off. "In the water, everyone. Looks like I got a head start."

Soon, his team were bobbing in the water beside him, adjusting air in their BCDs to descend. When Morgan landed beside him, she was grinning at him through her mask.

"I'll get revenge," he warned her.

She sank beneath the water, still smiling. Zach settled his mask in place and followed. It was probably wrong that he was enjoying tangling with her this much.

They all fell into the normal dive routine. The team started their search patterns, Alice and Max heading to study some of the locations of interest noted on their last dive.

As the dive progressed, they found more plates. It was promising, but it wasn't enough. Zach stared into the water all around him, listening to the rhythmic sound of his breathing. Where was the ship? What if she'd just been dropping goods for miles, before she broke up and went down? It could take months to find her, and they didn't have months. He knew they were running out of time.

He spotted Morgan swimming a few meters away, across a small ridge of rock. Fish darted out of her way.

As he watched, she stopped, floating with perfect buoyancy control, looking over the rocky ridge. That's when he saw her stiffen, then lean down and pluck something out of the rock. She turned and waved him over urgently.

Concerned, he kicked strongly and came up beside her.

She opened her palm, handing him what she'd picked up. He took it, turning it over with a frown. It was a rock. It was a cloudy color, different from the rock on the seafloor beneath them...

He froze. He suddenly realized what he was holding.

A diamond. A huge uncut diamond.

Morgan grinned at him, then punched him lightly in the shoulder. She pointed down past the rocky ridge and together they swam that way, scanning the sea floor a few meters below.

They both saw it at the same moment. He reached out and grabbed her hand, his heart knocking hard against his ribs.

There, a few meters below on the sandy bottom, was the outline of a ship. Rotting timbers and corroded cannons lay covered in sea growth.

He squeezed her hand and she squeezed back.

They'd found the *Soleil d'Orient.*

They both hung there in the water for a while, sharing that initial moment of discovery. It felt damn good to have her by his side. Finally, he looked back and waved to get the others' attention. Alice spotted him.

Soon, they were surrounded by the group. Even without being able to talk, the excitement was palpable. Everyone pointed and shared some high fives.

Max started snapping photos with the camera, but soon Morgan tapped her watch. No one wanted to leave, hell, Zach wanted to stay, but they had to head back to the *Nymph*.

Aboard the *Storm Nymph*, the excitement was infectious. Everyone was talking all at once. Charity was squealing and Max was doing a victory dance.

Zach pulled his tanks off, grinning at them all. He pulled his wet suit half way down, and shook the water out of his hair. Beside him, Morgan had done the same, that maddening bikini top showing off her shoulders and arms.

He didn't let himself think. As the others were busy talking, he grabbed Morgan's hand and dragged her around the storage rack.

"What the—?"

He pushed her up against the wall, crowding her body with his.

She smiled. It was slow and sexy. "Feeling a little frisky, are we, Dr. James?"

"Zach," he said.

"Congratulations on your find, *Zach*."

He leaned in closer, letting his lips drift across her cheek. "And it was our find."

"Our find," she murmured.

He pressed his mouth to hers. Her lips opened in an instant.

It was hard and wild. He pushed her up against the wall, cupping her breasts, trying to get more of the taste of her. She wrapped her long legs around his waist.

The feel of her set his blood alight. He knew without a doubt, he'd never get enough of her.

Zach groaned against her lips. He didn't know what was more exciting—discovering the shipwreck, or kissing Morgan Kincaid.

Chapter Eleven

Darcy Ward strode out of the cold, snowy morning and into her favorite coffee shop. The scent of roasting coffee beans and brewing coffee hit her in the face and she breathed deep. She stomped the snow off her boots, dusted it off her favorite red coat, then headed over to order.

The very cute, and rather young, barista took her order and gave her a long, flirty look. "Name?"

"Darcy."

"That's a pretty name."

If only you weren't twelve, buddy. She moved to the other end of the counter, pulling out her phone. She could check her emails while she waited.

She thought of Declan and the others, half a world away, diving in azure waters. Her nose wrinkled. She'd take sun and sand over snow any day. She saw an email from Dec and tapped it open. She grinned. They'd found the wreck of the *Soleil d'Orient.* Brilliant.

Then her smile slipped away. It was exciting, but the attacks not so. It sounded like Zach James could have been killed. It all had the hallmarks of Silk Road.

Darcy knew they had to find a way to stop the bastards. Back at the office, she was busy running searches on Constantine Phaulkon and this mysterious amulet. She hoped to hell there was nothing to the legend, and she could get the word out that it didn't exist and wasn't on the ship. And now Dec wanted her to look into all of the archeologists and students. She needed to check bank accounts for unusual sums of money and any links between them and Silk Road.

She looked up and noticed a guy waiting for his drink across from her, scrolling through his phone, too. Hmm, Mr. Businessman was wearing a nice suit and looked like he had a nice bod under there. Even better, he was definitely not twelve.

The barista set a takeout cup on the counter. "Skinny hazelnut latte."

Both she and Mr. Businessman reached for the latte at the same time, hands bumping.

"Oh, I'm sorry," Darcy said. Ooh, he was really nice-looking, in a clean-cut kind of way. He even had sexy wire-rimmed glasses on. "I don't know why they bother asking for our names and then don't use them."

"Please, you take it." He gestured to the coffee.

"No. You were here first—" she eyed the scrawl on the side of the cup "—Aaron."

He took the coffee with a smile. "Well, since you clearly have excellent taste in coffee, maybe we should sit and drink it together?"

She was about to answer when she felt someone step up behind her.

Mr. Businessman's smile evaporated, and his hands clenched on his coffee cup. "Or maybe not." He turned and hurried out of the coffee shop.

Every nerve in Darcy's body was twitching. She smelled cologne: crisp, clean, with a hint of lime. Her belly tightened.

She turned slowly, and found herself staring at a man's broad chest. It was covered in a crisp, white shirt that looked like it would never dare to wrinkle. He was wearing a dark-blue suit, and had one hand resting on a lean hip that pushed his jacket back just far enough to show a glimpse of his holster and handgun.

Darcy wrinkled her nose. Why did a gun and holster under a suit have to look so damn sexy?

She looked up. The rugged jaw with a hint of stubble wasn't quite handsome, but it rated interesting. And the green eyes were as direct and intense as always. "Special Agent Burke."

"Ms. Ward."

"What are you doing here?" *And why aren't you far, far away in Washington DC?*

"You left a message saying you needed to speak with me."

Her mouth dropped open. "I meant for you to *call*, not show up here."

His serious face didn't change. "I was in the area."

Of course he was. Even FBI agents couldn't just dash around the country as they pleased.

"Skinny hazelnut latte for Darcy," the barista called out.

Darcy pushed past Burke and grabbed her coffee. "Thanks."

The barista set another cup down beside hers. "Black Americano."

As Burke leaned forward, his shoulder brushed Darcy's as he grabbed his coffee. "Shall we sit?"

She sighed. She didn't see any way out of it. "Fine."

The coffee shop was busy this time of day, with office workers grabbing their caffeine before heading to their offices. There was one table left at the back, with two small chairs pushed close together.

As she slid in, hanging her handbag on the back of her chair, Agent Burke sat beside her. His hard thigh bumped hers and she barely stopped herself from jolting.

She'd always envisaged FBI agents as older, overweight, and balding. They spent a lot of time sitting behind a desk, so it seemed unfair that Alastair Burke looked the way he did.

"So, no art thieves for you to chase today?" she asked, sipping her latte.

She saw the faintest smile before his lips flattened. "It's a bit slow today."

Darcy was pretty sure the man had made a joke, but you couldn't tell by looking at him. Did he ever truly smile or laugh? Or just chill out? He was always so intense.

"You said you had information on Silk Road," he said.

"Yes." *Get down to business, get out.* That was a

good plan. "Sydney and I are pulling together everything we can on Silk Road. Mainly, we're following the money trail."

Burke leaned forward, frowning. "These are dangerous people, Darcy. People who'll kill with little compulsion in order to get what they want." He paused. "And to protect their secrets."

"We're being careful. Treasure Hunter Security has already been targeted by this group. We want to help bring them down. Besides, I'm safe in my warehouse."

Burke's frown deepened. "They could hack your system and find a way in. I did."

And she was still mad about that. She'd spent a hell of a long time lately adding extra security measures to her system. She shot him a smug smile. "Bet you can't now."

He sighed. "What have you found?"

She pulled her slim tablet out of her bag. She tapped, pulled up the information, and turned it around for him to see. She scrolled through the pages. "London is a hub for them. And we believe they have three top people."

Burke eyed her, shifting closer. "Why three?"

She got another whiff of his cologne, and her belly twisted in knots. *Focus, Darce. Jeez.* Obviously, his team hadn't discovered this information yet. That made her feel good. "Whenever money comes in to pay for something, it comes in threes. And I've managed to find a couple of black market sales of stolen antiquities that I can attribute to Silk Road. The money all went out in threes, too."

"Black market sales?" His gaze narrowed. "You know hacking is illegal."

She straightened and put on an innocent face. "Of course."

Another sigh. "This is good work."

Darcy told herself not to feel so happy about his praise. "I also got a name of someone who I think is one of the higher-ranked people in the group. A Dr. Paris Wirth."

Now Burke stiffened. He reached out and grabbed Darcy's wrist. "You leave this investigation alone now, Darcy. I'll take it from here."

She ignored the order. "Who is he?"

"She." Burke lifted his hand, running it over his hair. "She's dangerous, cold, and calculating. She's been flagged several times by my team, but no one's been able to definitively link her to Silk Road. She's obsessed with finding artifacts, especially ones she believes hold power. And she won't hesitate to kill to get what she wants."

A small shiver of fear ran up Darcy's spine. "Sounds like a fun gal."

"Send me the data you have, and I'll look over it."

"I'll email it—" She pulled the tablet toward her.

His hand covered hers again, surprising her. It was way bigger than hers, with blunt fingers and neatly clipped nails. It was also warm, and she felt that small touch all the way through her body.

"No," he said. "I'll give you access to upload to one of my secure servers. It'll be safer."

That sounded good. She slowly pulled her hand away from his disturbing touch. If he let her into his server, she could have a little peek around in there while she was uploading her files.

Now he smiled. It wasn't a big, beaming smile, but it turned that dark, intense face into something eye-catching. "I don't keep anything important on there."

She grabbed her latte and took a sip. "I don't know what you're talking about, Agent Burke."

"I'm sure you don't." He stood, his suit jacket falling back into place.

Darcy looked up at him, her gaze on his stomach. She was pretty sure she could see faint ridges of hard abs beneath his shirt. Then she straightened. *Shit, don't look at his abs, Darcy. This is Agent Arrogant and Annoying, the bane of your existence.*

"Well, we finally had a cordial conversation," he said. "And coffee together."

He made it sound like they'd been on a date. "Guess it's feeling rather chilly in Hell today."

That faint smile again. "Back off on the Silk Road research, Darcy."

And Hell was back to a blazing inferno. "I'm not doing anything illegal, Agent Burke." She stood now, grabbing her bag and slinging it over her shoulder.

She circled the table, but he stepped in front of her, blocking her way. His hand circled her arm and people leaving the next table jostled them, pushing them close together.

"Listen to me—" he growled.

She looked into that intense face and saw something hot in his eyes.

"You *will* stay away from Silk Road."

"Giving orders probably works for your subordinates. My brothers have tried the orders and demands thing, too." She shot him a sweet smile. "Doesn't work for them, either."

Burke leaned down close, his warm breath brushing over her cheek. "I don't want that pretty ass of yours getting hurt."

He'd noticed her ass? She didn't let herself dwell on that, and, instead, drew herself up. It was a shame he was bossy, overbearing, and arrogant. "I can take care of my own ass." She patted her hand against his chest. "Have a safe trip back to DC, Agent Burke."

***

Zach and his team were diving, but Morgan had stayed on deck to keep an eye on things. Dec and Coop had gone down with the archeologists. She spotted Hale walking on the balcony surrounding the bridge and gave him a nod.

She eyed the clouds gathering in the sky, and then glanced down at the choppy waves. It was nothing to be worried about yet, but she planned to keep an eye on it. Then, her gaze snagged on a boat hanging around in the distance, back toward Tolagnaro. It had been there for the last hour. She frowned, then turned and climbed up the steps to the bridge.

She caught Hale's gaze. "You see that boat?"

"Yep. Definitely watching us."

She walked onto the bridge. Diego was looking out the window with a set of binoculars. "You've noticed the boat."

"I see them," the man answered. "Local fishing boat, but there are also a few foreigners on board."

Morgan paused beside him, looking out the window. "Treasure hunters?"

Diego nodded. "Be my guess. People in town are bound to talk. They saw us come in, gather supplies, and leave port."

She considered the boat. "If it was Silk Road, we wouldn't see them. Keep an eye on the vessel, and if they come any closer or put anyone in the water, let me know."

"You got it. I'm more worried about the storm coming in. It's looking like it will pass to the west of us, though."

She looked at the sullen clouds. "Keep me posted on that, as well."

Morgan headed back out onto the deck and her watch beeped. The divers should be back now. A few seconds later, she saw heads popping out of the water beside the *Nymph*.

Blondie and her friend were talking a mile a minute. Morgan reached down and gripped Charity's hand, pulling her up, then Jasmin. Morgan helped them out of their tanks. "What did you guys find?"

Charity wrung out her ponytail. "It was *so* amazing—"

Zach's head broke the surface and he shoved his mask up. "We need the ROV with the salvage arm." He was grinning at her.

Damn him for having those sexy dimples. "What did you find?"

"Some chests."

She remembered the manifest. Chest of diamonds. Zach pulled himself out, water streaming down his body.

She turned and saw Marc nearby. "We need the ROV. The big one."

The man nodded. "I'll get her ready."

As the divers all got their gear off, Marc and Turner got the ROV prepped. Soon, Oceanid was loaded onto the crane arm.

Morgan stacked empty tanks, and then set new ones out. A small team of divers was planning to accompany the ROV. The next batch of divers suited up, ready to go in with Oceanid. This time Taye, Max, Coop and Hale were going down.

The crane arm slowly swung out over the side of the ship, and then the ROV was lowered into the water. The divers entered, and soon, they all disappeared beneath the choppy waves.

Oceanid had to be controlled from the computer room, and Morgan found Diego in a big, battered chair, in front of a large screen displaying a live feed from under the water. His hands rested on two control joysticks.

Morgan leaned against the wall to watch.

Moments later, Zach appeared. He was in khaki shorts and a tight, black T-shirt, and his hair was damp. He was vibrating with energy.

She shook her head. The man really loved his adventures.

On the screen, she saw the divers moving ahead. She frowned. Visibility had really dropped, thanks to the weather.

"The location of the chests is on the port side of the wreck," Zach said. "You'll want to move a little to the left."

Diego nodded, and the ROV turned smoothly. Then the divers paused, clustered around a point. One of them was pointing.

The ROV's camera moved, and Morgan leaned forward, staring at the screen.

"There it is," Zach said.

She tried to pick anything out of the murky image, but it all looked like dark shadows to her. Zach pointed over her shoulder.

"Look." His lips brushed her ear.

She shivered briefly, and then she spotted them. The distinct, rectangular shapes of two chests.

"Okay, we'll use the arm and get these loaded up. Marc knows what to do." Diego's gaze never left the screen. He concentrated on the controls, moving the arms, and working with Marc below. Soon, they got the first chest loaded. They were working on the second one, when one of the divers held up a hand for them to pause.

The divers were all looking at something.

"What do you think they spotted?" Morgan asked.

Zach shrugged and winked. "No idea. All part of the adventure."

A second later, the divers moved back and one of them—Marc—pointed downward.

"Can you get a better view?" Zach asked.

"Hang on." Diego's brow was furrowed. "There."

Morgan squinted at the image. "Another smaller chest."

"More of a box," Zach murmured.

They watched as the divers got the smaller chest loaded. Soon, the divers and the ROV were making their way back up to the ship.

Morgan and Zach headed back out on deck, waiting by the railing for them to appear.

"You look like a kid at Christmas," she said.

Zach glanced at her. "I doubt it. I never got any Christmas gifts as a kid. I bet this is way better than something wrapped in gaudy paper."

Those simple words were a punch to her chest. He'd never gotten a Christmas gift? Her father had always made a big effort to get her what she wanted. It made her smile even now to think of the hard Marine going doll shopping. Sure, once she was older, it had morphed into knife shopping. But in the early years, he'd bought her dresses and dolls.

She'd been lucky. Luckier than she'd realized. After her father was killed, she'd spent so long being angry. Hell, some days she was still angry. She'd lost the one person who'd loved her unconditionally, for all her sharp edges. Maybe it was finally time to come to terms with that.

She glanced at Zach, with his lust for life and passion for his work. He'd made something of himself from nothing, with no one to support him.

Suddenly, Oceanid broke the water's surface, bobbing in the swell. Marc appeared beside it, hooking it onto the crane arm. Morgan waved to Turner, and the young man activated the crane controls. The ROV lifted out of the water, and was swung over onto the deck. By the time they had it disconnected, the divers were out of the water and peeling off their wet suits.

Zach directed his team, and they carefully unloaded the chests from the ROV, and whisked them away to the wet lab.

"Be careful." Zach hovered beside them, as they moved the chests up the stairs.

Morgan followed the archeologists into the wet lab. Everyone packed into the room, watching eagerly as each chest was set in a tray. Zach went to work on one chest, taking photos of it before he snapped on gloves and started to touch it. Alice was working on the other chest.

They all waited with bated breath. Dec arrived, leaning against the wall with Morgan. "This is the exciting bit."

She nodded, but actually, she thought the exciting bit was watching Zach's face as he carefully opened the lid of his chest.

He sucked in a sharp breath, and beside him, Charity's mouth dropped open.

"Oh, my sweet Lord—" the young woman murmured.

Someone let out a whistle.

Morgan and Dec moved forward, craning their necks to look into the chest.

Jesus. It was filled with uncut diamonds.

Everyone started cheering.

Zach lifted his head, grinning. "This is a piece of history, people. Have some respect." His gaze met Morgan's and he winked.

"Those are some big-ass diamonds!" Hale said.

Alice opened the second chest. The archeologist broke into a smile. "Gold coins."

The coins had been dulled by the hundreds of years spent lost in the ocean, but Morgan saw the muted glint of gold inside the box.

"Okay, I need you guys to get to work." Zach's tone turned serious. "I need all this documented, and the coins need to be cleaned."

As his team moved into action, full of cheerful chatter, Zach lifted the smaller box that had been brought up into another tray. It was nowhere as large as the chests, and only a few inches high.

Morgan moved closer, peering over his shoulder. "I don't think there are any diamonds in there."

"I don't care. It will still be something interesting, and another piece of the puzzle of the *Soleil d'Orient's* story." Zach looked at the box exactly the same way he'd looked at the other chests. It didn't matter to him if it was diamonds or gold, or shards of pots or plates. Everything was equally as important.

He wiped a soft cloth over the box, uncovering a metal binding that was inlaid into the wood. Leaning forward, focused, he kept cleaning. "I think there's writing on this."

He wiped again and stiffened.

"What?" She looked at the faint etchings on the metal, and her breath caught. "Is that Greek?"

Zach nodded, moving his gloved finger reverently over the text. "It's a name. Constantine Phaulkon."

From beside her, Morgan sensed Declan straighten. Zach's gaze met Morgan's.

She nodded. "Open it."

He lifted the lid.

Morgan frowned, the air rushing out of her in a disappointed whoosh. The box was empty.

Chapter Twelve

Zach sat at a table in the galley with the THS team. Outside, the sun was setting, the western horizon awash in orange. The storm that had been threatening had passed.

The Phaulkon case had been empty, but he'd spent several hours studying it. The bottom had a carved hollow in the center of it, which looked like a place for a pendant on a chain to rest.

"Maybe someone was wearing the pendant when the ship went down?" Morgan suggested. "We could still find it down there."

He nodded. He knew he should be excited. He'd proved that there was a pendant—whether it was a powerful amulet was still up for discussion.

"I suggest you make the find public," Dec said.

Zach's head snapped up. "What? And have every treasure hunter in the southern hemisphere all over us? There are still more artifacts down there."

"But none of them are worth anyone's life. If we announce that we found some artifacts belonging to Phaulkon and we've sent them away for safekeeping, it might stop Silk Road from sniffing around here. Sure, we'll have to deal with amateur treasure hunters, but at least they won't kill anyone."

"You want to lie," Zach said.

Declan raised a brow. "Well, this box belonged to Phaulkon, so technically we aren't lying. We'll leave it up to Silk Road to assume we found the Phaulkon amulet."

Morgan nodded, resting her clasped hands on the table. "Take away the one thing Silk Road wants, and they go away."

Cooper shifted. "Is Darcy having any luck tracking Silk Road?"

"Some," Declan said. "She met with Burke from the FBI. They're following some angles, and she's identified one possible high-ranking member. Apparently, an obsessive artifact hunter named Dr. Paris Wirth, who has a thing for artifacts that are reputed to have power. Oh, and she's also a ruthless killer."

Morgan grimaced. "Nice."

The last thing Zach wanted was ruthless killers on board.

"Zach," Declan said. "I need to ask if any of your team are acting out of character."

Zach frowned. "What? Why?"

The man's gray eyes were steady and serious. "We believe the person who attacked you was a member of your team."

Heat shot through Zach and he shook his head. "No. I've worked with Alice and Taye for years. They're my friends. The students I don't know as well, but none of them strike me as being capable of murder."

Declan sighed. "You'd be surprised what people are capable of, given the right motivation."

Dammit. Zach released a long breath. The last thing he wanted was to suspect his team.

"I have my sister digging into everyone's background. Nothing's popped as yet."

"And we have another problem," Morgan said. "If we have a Silk Road informant on board, then they know we haven't found the amulet."

Zach ran a hand through his hair. "Well, I can tell my team that I did some more work on the Phaulkon box...and discovered the amulet. They'll believe me." He hated the thought of lying to them, but if it kept them alive, he'd do it. He glanced at Morgan. "Okay. If you all think it's the safest thing to do, we'll announce the discovery and send some artifacts back to Denver."

Declan nodded and stood. "I'll talk to Darcy to arrange secure transport." He looked at Hale and Coop. "You two are on watch."

Morgan stayed behind, and Zach turned to watch the last of the beautiful sunset. Africa was somewhere that way, beyond the horizon. He imagined what it must have been like to be the captain of an East Indiaman like the *Soleil d'Orient.* Sailing through uncharted waters, circling the dark continent back before it had been fully explored.

Zach sighed. He'd wanted to find the amulet. He didn't believe it had special powers, but to hold something that had sat around the neck of an adventurer like Phaulkon would have been amazing.

Whatever happened, whatever else they found on the wreck, he wasn't letting Silk Road hurt anyone else.

"You should be thrilled," Morgan said. "Chests of diamonds and gold are a pretty amazing find."

"I am happy."

"You're just not happy that the Phaulkon box was empty."

Damn, she could obviously read him like an open book. "I wanted the amulet to be there."

"We'll keep looking. It's not over yet, Dr. James."

"And if one of my team is a traitor? If Silk Road comes back?"

Her mouth hardened. "Then they'll wish they hadn't."

Because she'd fight them. She'd put herself between him and his team to protect them. What if she got hurt? What if Declan and the others got hurt?

Morgan wasn't watching the dying sun. Instead, she was staring toward the dark shore. She frowned. "There's no record of any survivors from the *Soleil d'Orient*?"

"No."

"But she went down quite close to the shore, and quite close to Fort Dauphin. If someone had made it to shore, they could've easily gotten back to the settlement."

"No survivors were found. It was apparently a violent storm."

She looked over at him. "What if a few people did make it to shore? Perhaps carrying important things?"

Zach stared at the silhouetted shoreline. "I guess they could've made it, but didn't survive long enough to make it to Fort Dauphin. It's not likely, but it's possible."

"It's worth a look," she said.

"Yeah. It's worth a look. I'm going to head back to the lab and take another look at the Phaulkon box."

"I'll give you a hand."

In the lab, Zach soon found himself absorbed in his work. This box had been Phaulkon's, held in the man's hands. Zach leaned over, making some notations in his notebook. A noise made him look up. He blinked at Morgan.

He'd forgotten she was there. She leaned against the bench, watching him with a smile.

Shit, he'd lost track of time. He knew it was late. "Sorry." His tone was sheepish. "I zoned out, didn't I?"

"You're kind of cute when you're all nerdy."

"I'm not nerdy." He remembered the name-calling at school. He'd vowed that no one would ever call him a nerd again.

She smiled, circling the bench and grabbing the front of his shirt. "It's sexy. I never thought the sexy professor thing worked for me."

His blood heated and went straight to his cock.

She smelled like woman and Morgan. "And now?"

She pressed up against him. "Now, I find it a little appealing."

He gripped her waist and lifted her up onto the bench. He nudged her legs apart and stepped between them. "Only a little?"

She tipped her head back. "Maybe more than that. But I might still need some convincing."

He kissed her, a tangling of tongues and teeth. Her hands slid into his hair, tugging hard. He thrust his tongue inside her mouth and her tongue met his. He drank in the taste of her.

When he pulled back, he was panting. "Jesus, Morgan, you fry my brain cells."

She slid her hands across his shoulders, licking her lips. "Lucky you have so many of them, then. That's what got me all hot and bothered, watching you work. You looked so serious and dedicated."

He kissed her again—slow, wet, and hard. She sank her teeth into his bottom lip, and growled. He *had* to touch her. He slid his hands up under her T-shirt, stroking her firm belly. Then his hands went lower and he flicked open the button on her trousers. "I can't wait to touch you. Feel how wet you are."

"Yes." She lifted her hips to give him better access.

Distracted by the feel of her breast under his hand, he pinched at her nipple.

With a growl, she grabbed his hand and slid it inside her trousers.

He laughed. "So demanding."

"Stop talking and touch me."

He slid his fingers through the curls he found. "Slick."

"God, yes," she purred.

"All for me."

Her eyes met his, wide open and filled with need. "All for you."

He yanked her right to the edge of the bench to give him better access. Desire was riding him hard, and he was struck by the fantasy of her naked body laid out on a big bed. Those long legs clenched around his hips as he slid inside her.

Zach growled and found her clit, rolling it between his fingers. She jerked against him, her mouth open, her breath coming in pants.

He slid his mouth down her neck, tasting the faint flavor of salt on her skin. He sucked a little, and at the same time, slid his fingers down to where she was plump and damp. He pushed two fingers inside her.

She nearly came off the bench, her hips lifting. "*Yes*, Zach."

The sound of his name made him smile, satisfaction a hard knot in his chest. He kept working her, sliding his thumb up to rub her swollen clit. He wanted to see her come. He needed to see her come.

"You want me."

"Yes."

"You need me."

"Yes, Zach. Please."

He loved the sound of need and felt she was

nearing the edge. Then he felt her body clench, and color suffused her cheeks. She threw her head back and made a husky cry as she came.

Damn. Zach had never seen anything more beautiful.

She dropped her head forward and it landed against his shoulder. As he pulled his fingers out of her, she moaned. He lifted his hand and licked at the juices she'd left there.

He saw heat spike in her eyes again. His cock was like solid rock, pressing mercilessly against his zipper. "Morgan, I've never wanted anything as much as I want to thrust my cock inside you and feel you wrapped around me."

She groaned. "I want that. I do. But I've got watch in ten minutes. I have to take over from Hale."

Now it was Zach's turn to groan.

She kissed his jaw, nipping at him. "Dream of me?"

"Yes." He could barely think of anything else.

Her mouth skated to his earlobe. "Think of my mouth traveling down this lovely, lean body of yours. I want to lick every muscle." Her fingers skimmed to his waistband, drifting over the bulge of his cock. "I want to suck this inside my mouth and drive you crazy."

Zach shuddered, his hands clenching on her. "You trying to kill me?"

"Not today, Dr. James." She slid off the bench, fastening her trousers. "I have plans for you."

He watched the subtle swing of her hips as she

walked out, leaving him hard and wanting.

***

Morgan kept a steady hand on the controls of the small inflatable boat as she and Zach zoomed toward the shore. She glanced at him to make sure he was holding on. They crested a wave and came down hard.

There was another storm gathering on the horizon, clouds brewing. She made a mental note to check the weather again with Diego when they got back to the ship.

She'd told Dec that she was taking Zach to do a recon of the shoreline. If her theory that perhaps survivors had made it to shore was true, they might find some evidence of it. She knew Zach had spent the morning telling his team he'd found the amulet. Lying to them wouldn't have been easy for him.

They rode some more waves in, and finally, she aimed the boat toward a sandy spot free of rocks. As the boat nosed up onto the sand, she throttled back the engine and turned it off. Zach got out, splashing through the ankle-deep water to grab the front of the boat. Together, they pulled it farther up on the sand.

The shore was quite pretty here. A small, sandy stretch of beach nestled under a large hill, with not too much vegetation, and some rocky outcrops. As she straightened, she looked at Zach. They hadn't had much of a chance to talk since last night. But just looking at the way his T-shirt stretched over his chest made her think of that moment in the lab, when he'd had his clever fingers inside her and his tongue in her mouth.

Like he'd read her thoughts, he grabbed her, and yanked her in for a hard kiss.

She pressed her hands to his back. God, he tasted so good. "They could see us from the boat."

He made a frustrated sound and stepped back a few inches. "Right. Sorry. Just a little worked up." He shot her a heated look. "I didn't sleep well."

She walked up onto the shore. "Don't worry, we'll tangle, Dr. James."

He groaned again. "Promise?"

"Promise. I like sex."

His face looked strangely blank. "I like sex, too."

"Good. And it'll be just sex."

"Okay," he said slowly.

"I have rules. I don't need any handholding."

He put on a mock look of horror. "Perish the thought."

"And if you try and hold a door for me, or carry my bag, I will hurt you."

He held his hands up. "You can carry your own bags. Got it."

"Good." They reached a rocky outcrop, and she roughly pulled him around. Once out of view of the ship, she nudged him until his back hit the rock. She went up on her toes and pressed her mouth to his.

He deepened the kiss and it turned hot, honest, and raw. He clasped the back of her head, and her fingers twisted in his T-shirt.

She pulled back a little, breathing fast. "Other than those rules I mentioned, anything goes." God, the man made her forget herself. Forget that she was currently working.

He groaned. "Something tells me that hard, fast sex in the sand right now isn't on the menu."

She stepped back, patting his cheek. "You do not want sand in hard-to-reach, uncomfortable places. Come on, Dr. James. We've got some exploring to do."

They walked along the shore, moving toward the rocky side of the hill.

Morgan glanced at him. Yes, when they got off the ship, they'd have some fun. Eventually, they'd need to head in to Tolagnaro for supplies. She had plans to lock herself and Zach in a hotel room for a day and work off this raging desire. Hmm, maybe a couple of days.

It would burn out. They'd have a great time, finish this job, and then he'd flit off on his next adventure. The heat would fade. It always did.

Or, her sharper edges wouldn't be so fascinating for him anymore. That always happened. She was always too tall, too strong, too tough.

Work to do, Morgan. She forced herself to focus and stared back out to sea. She quickly found the solid, white shape of the *Storm Nymph*. "This is the most direct line from where the ship sank, to the shore." She studied the shoreline. "If survivors made it, they'd look for shelter." She spotted an opening in the cliff ahead. "Looks like there are caves along here."

"Well, there are plenty of caves all over Madagascar. In the north, there is a reserve especially for the longest cave system on the island, and some think it's the longest in all of Africa. It's sacred to the local people, and the caves have been used for shelter and protection for years. And not too far from here, a group of paleontologists found fossils of extinct animals in flooded caves."

Morgan stepped over some rocks, moving closer to the cliff face. "Oh?"

"Yes. The researchers found the bones of horned crocodiles, pygmy hippos, giant elephant birds, and giant lemurs the size of gorillas."

"I think I prefer the cute, small lemurs we have today."

"Those flooded freshwater caves were found in a national park about two hundred and fifty miles from here. I hear it's an amazing place."

She guessed this voice was the one he used on his students. "If any survivors made it to shore, they would have been exhausted, scared, possibly injured. They wouldn't have gone far." She studied the mouth of a nearby cave. "Makes sense that they'd hole up somewhere and regroup."

"By the time the *Soleil d'Orient* went down, the French were gone, ousted by the locals. If the local Malagasy spotted them, they may have been hostile."

They stepped into the cave. The very empty cave.

Morgan pulled out a flashlight and flicked it on.

She aimed it around the dark spaces and walls.

"No historic amulets?" he asked.

"Sorry, no. No giant lemurs, either."

"Even if someone made it, they could have sheltered anywhere along the coast here."

Morgan moved back to the cave mouth and glanced at the worsening clouds in the sky. "Weather is coming in. We'll have to cut this short, if you still want to get one more dive in before the storm hits."

"Okay." When they turned back toward the boat, he grabbed her hand, linking their fingers.

Morgan looked down at their joined hands with a narrowed gaze. "Zach—"

He grinned at her. "It's not handholding. This is helping a friend across rocky ground."

"Do I look like I need help?"

"No, you most definitely do not. But I do." He tightened his grip, shooting her his most charming grin, dimples flashing. "It's your job to keep me safe. You said so yourself."

She shook her head. Tricky, charming rogue. Warmth flooded her chest, even as unease tickled along her spine. Morgan wondered just how she was going to protect her heart from Zach James.

Chapter Thirteen

By the time Zach and Morgan got back to the *Storm Nymph*, the sea was getting rough. The ship was rocking wildly, and as he strode out on deck, Zach saw all three of his students leaning over the side, emptying their stomachs.

He glanced at Taye and they shared a smile. He remembered his first underwater archeology dive. He'd spent a fair bit of time feeding the fish, as well.

Morgan headed straight for the dive gear. She moved across the rolling deck without a hitch in her stride, like it didn't affect her at all.

"I suggest we do a shorter dive." She looked at her heavy-duty dive watch. "We don't want to get caught in the storm."

He nodded, pulling on his suit and tanks. As the deck pitched, he widened his stance. "Like the *Soleil d'Orient.*" He imagined what it would have been like back then to be standing on the deck of the ship as it broke apart. Panicked people running and jumping over the edge. The captain standing at the helm, desolation and horror spreading through him as he realized his ship was going down.

Morgan bumped her hip against Zach's. "Hey? Let's move it, Dr. James."

In the water, visibility had decreased significantly. The last few days of diving had instilled the routine in everyone and the team moved with precision as they headed toward the wreck.

Soon, everyone was working, combing through the search areas, taking photographs, collecting artifacts. Zach wondered if the Phaulkon amulet was somewhere here, covered by sand.

Morgan joined him, tapping her watch. She held up her hand to indicate five minutes. He nodded.

Suddenly, arms wrapped around him from behind, jerking him backward. Shock was a storm to his system, bubbles covering the front of his mask.

He turned his head and caught a glimpse of a diver wearing a silver wet suit that made him almost invisible in the murky water. Movement nearby caught his attention. Another silver-suited person was trying to subdue Morgan. She was fighting in a wild struggle.

Zach jerked his body, and slammed an elbow at his attacker. He saw the two divers were pulling him and Morgan away from their group.

Soon, the wreck and their team disappeared in the murkiness. Zach swung an arm, trying to wrench free. Then he felt a prick on the side of his neck.

What the hell? He swung again, his regulator slipping from his mouth. Instantly, he started to feel woozy. He looked over and saw that Morgan was already hanging limp in the water.

No! He tried to struggle, but he felt the strength leaking from his limbs. Someone shoved the regulator back in his mouth.

Be okay, Morgan. She had to be okay. Then everything faded into black.

Zach felt himself drifting. He heard an engine, sensed the world bobbing beneath him, and felt the wind in his face.

He had no idea how much time had passed, but finally, he fought through the fog and opened his eyes.

His head was throbbing and he groggily lifted it. He was being half carried, half dragged, then dropped roughly on the ground. Rocks bit into him and he groaned. He looked around. They were on the shore, at the mouth of a cave, and rain was splattering around them.

Morgan was dropped beside him. She fell in a slump and didn't move.

"Morgan." He reached over, pushing her damp hair back. *God, please be alive.*

"She'll wake up shortly," a clipped voice said. "The drugs will wear off soon."

Two muscular men in silver wet suits stood over them. Behind them was a wall of gray rain and crashing waves.

"Who are you?" Zach demanded.

The closest man shook his head. "We wait for the boss."

Great. That's when he noticed Morgan's

breathing was labored. His chest tightened and he touched her cheek.

Her skin was deathly pale and she was restless. With each breath, she was wheezing, like she was having trouble breathing.

"Something's wrong." Sheer panic coursed through him. He touched her wrist and felt that her pulse was weak. "She can't breathe!"

Help her. Protect her. His vision dimmed, his sole focus on Morgan. From the moment he'd met her, she'd been vibrant, filled with life, and so strong. A part of him had thought her invulnerable.

As she wheezed for air, her lashes dark against her pale cheeks, fear rose to choke him like rusty wire against his throat. He gripped her hand. She wasn't superwoman. "Morgan! You hang in there."

One of the guards cursed and knelt on the other side of her. "A fucking allergic reaction to the drugs."

"Help her!" Zach spied the man fingering something on his belt.

A small first aid kit.

Zach leaped forward and yanked the kit away.

"Hey!" The guard reached out to snatch it back.

"Boss wanted them alive," the other guard said.

Zach ignored them, fueled by the harsh sound of Morgan's breathing. He tore the kit open, and a second later, spied the pre-filled injection pen filled with epinephrine. He tore it open and stabbed it into Morgan's thigh, through her wet suit.

She groaned, her head turning to the side. He discarded the pen and pulled her closer. He held her, every labored breath scratching over his nerves, but within a few minutes, he heard her breathing ease.

Morgan's eyelids fluttered and he saw her looking at him.

"Jesus Christ, Morgan." His pulse was still racing. He pulled her closer. "Are you okay?"

She blinked and sagged back against him. "Okay."

Something tight and hot inside him eased. He still felt like he'd swallowed a rock, a lump in his throat, but she was okay.

As she closed her eyes, he realized just what it took for a woman like Morgan to let herself relax in his arms. To trust him to protect her.

Morgan was the strongest, toughest, most stubborn woman he'd ever met. And he'd almost lost her. The air shuddered out of him. In a moment of clarity, he realized just how much she meant to him, and how much more he wanted.

The guards were murmuring amongst themselves, but Zach ignored them. Until she was conscious, he'd take care of her.

"Dr. James, it is a pleasure to meet you."

It was a woman's voice with a sharp British accent. He looked up.

The woman was tiny, under five feet, wearing khaki outdoor gear. She had a cute face and her hair fell in a neat blonde bob. She was flanked by two more guards wearing all-black gear. They were tall and muscular as well. All ex-military, if he had to guess, and none of them looked particularly friendly.

"Who are you?" Zach pulled Morgan closer to him. "What are—?"

The woman smiled, shaking her head. "You don't get to ask questions, Dr. James, I do. I have to tell you that I've read some of your papers. Your work is very good."

She was talking to him like they were meeting at a conference. "Okay."

Another pleasant smile. "Now, where's the Phaulkon amulet?"

Zach was silent for a moment. "I found the amulet in a box with Phaulkon's name engraved on it. It's been sent back to my museum in Denver."

The woman tapped a finger to her lips. "No. I don't believe that. I was informed the box was empty."

Damn, someone on the ship *was* spying. "Who told you?" Anger was a violent rush through his veins.

The woman smiled. "Always the last person you'd expect. Loyalty is a hard commodity to earn and far, far easier to buy." She lifted a gun, and pointed it at Morgan. "You just have to find the right currency."

Zach's heart spasmed, and he shifted in front of Morgan's prone form. "You'd kill an innocent woman?"

"I do whatever is required to get the job done. I would think a true guardian of history like you would understand that."

Zach evaluated his options. There was a light in her eyes. Something hot and covetous. He'd seen the same look in the eyes of other archeologists on the hunt. Hell, he'd seen it in his own eyes once or twice.

But this woman had something deeper and much colder in her gaze.

She'd do whatever it took to get what she wanted. And that included killing Morgan.

He had to do something to protect the woman in his arms.

"I have no idea where the amulet is. We did find a box but, yes, it was empty. Look, you want the truth...I doubt the amulet ever existed, and even if it did, it's just an artifact."

The woman shook her head. "Oh, we both know it's much more than that."

Beneath his hands, he felt Morgan's body tighten. He realized she was awake, but not giving it away. He needed to tell her what was going on.

"So, you and your four goons are after the amulet. Look, it's probably lost forever out there." He waved a hand toward the churning ocean. "It was probably around the neck of some poor victim claimed by the sea."

"I very much doubt some lackey was wearing the amulet," the woman answered. "But I know they protected it. And I think you came ashore earlier today because you agree with my theory."

Zach stiffened. "Can you put the gun away, please? And sure, tell me your theory."

The gun didn't waver. "Someone brought the amulet ashore."

"There's no way to prove that."

The guard nearest to Zach kicked him. As pain exploded in his side, Zach grunted.

"Show some respect and answer the doctor's questions," the guard growled.

Suddenly, Morgan moved with the speed of a striking cobra. She grabbed the man's ankle, and twisted it violently. The man yelled as he fell. A second guard rushed forward, but Morgan spun, and rammed her fist up under the man's jaw. His head snapped back and she slammed a fist into his gut. He fell backward and landed on the first downed man.

"You hurt him, I'll make you pay." Morgan's voice was low and deadly.

The blonde woman stepped forward, her gun aimed at Morgan's chest. "I don't believe you are faster than a bullet, Miss Kincaid."

Morgan eyed the woman up and down and Zach saw Morgan tense up even more. "You're Paris Wirth."

The woman smiled. "You've heard of me. Lovely. And it is *Dr.* Paris Wirth."

Morgan nodded. "I've heard you're an unstable, thieving killer."

Wirth's smile morphed into a scowl. "Bitch."

"I haven't even gotten started yet," Morgan said. "Oh, I also know that Silk Road pulls your strings."

"You don't know what you're talking about," Wirth said. "And it is an honor to work for a forward-thinking group like Silk Road. Now, I want the amulet."

Zach caught Morgan's gaze. They had to get away from this woman.

"Now, Dr. James," Wirth said. "You are going to help me find the Phaulkon amulet." The woman's gaze flicked to Morgan. "But Miss Kincaid, I think you're just going to be a dangerous problem I don't need." She took another step forward and lifted her gun to aim between Morgan's eyes.

Fuck. Zach moved fast, shoving his body between Morgan and the gun. "No!"

***

Morgan's heart was lodged in her throat. She grabbed Zach's shoulders, frightened that at any second she'd hear the gun go off.

She was terrified that he'd die in a hail of bullets, just like her father. That she'd be forced to watch all that vibrant life and cheeky charm drain from his eyes.

Zach threw an arm out in front of her. "Morgan is simply hired security. Killing her gains nothing and certainly won't guarantee my help."

She went still, watching his face carefully. He was...smiling at Wirth.

"You are an educated woman," he told Wirth. "I can see that. I'm interested to hear your information and theories." Those dimples flashed. "Perhaps if we pool our intelligence, we can find the amulet. Together."

He was…flirting with the woman? A sour taste filled Morgan's mouth.

Wirth smiled, color in her cheeks. "I'd like that. I can see you're an intelligent man with similar interests to me."

He nodded. "Exactly. Morgan here isn't really into history. She's hired muscle."

"It must have been tough for you to be stuck with uneducated people who can't match your intellect."

As Zach nodded, an arrow shot through Morgan's chest.

"Morgan's been an interesting diversion." He glanced at her and she searched his face for any hint of truth. This was all for Wirth's benefit, wasn't it?

But she saw nothing but polite apology on his handsome features. Ice slid through her and she wiped her face blank of emotion, pulling inward.

Stay alive. That was all that mattered right now. He didn't look her way, his gaze seemingly glued to the pert Dr. Wirth.

"But we're civilized people," Zach continued. "There's no need for bloodshed. I'm sure Morgan will not step out of line."

Paris Wirth made a small noise and lowered the gun. "Fine. But—" she skewered Morgan with a hard stare "—you step out of line, and I'll put a bullet in Dr. James. Then I'll make you watch him bleed out—slowly and painfully."

Morgan's hand flexed.

"That's how your father died, isn't it?" Wirth

said with a sly smile.

Morgan surged forward, but Zach grabbed her. As soon as she got the chance, Morgan was taking this woman down. She jerked away from his touch. "Let me go."

"Do you understand me, Miss Kincaid?" Wirth asked.

"Understood." Morgan pushed the word out from between clenched teeth.

Zach shifted, but Morgan couldn't bring herself to look at him. He was exactly what she suspected. A big fat liar.

Morgan did what she did best, and kept her gaze on the danger in front of them. Zach might not be the man she'd thought he was, but it was her job to keep him safe. Even if she wanted to hurt him herself, she'd keep him safe.

Zach cleared his throat. "Dr. Wirth, I really don't understand how I can help you find the amulet—"

"Please, call me Paris." Wirth held up a hand, then jerked her head at her guards. One of the goons moved forward, nudging Zach toward a nearby cave.

A second guard grabbed Morgan's arm and pushed her forward with a shove. He had a graze on his face from where she'd knocked him over, and his dark eyes promised retribution.

Surely, she and Zach would have been missed by now. Declan would be looking for them.

They were forced to the mouth the cave. It looked similar to the one they'd explored today, just a little larger. The guards marched them up to a rock wall.

A flashlight clicked on, illuminating the wall.

Morgan stared at the smooth rock. What the hell did this woman want? A miracle?

Then Zach made a sound. She turned and saw his face, and the amazement etched on it. For a second, she stared at that handsome face she'd admired so much over the last few days. Pain stabbed at her and she turned back, and this time, she spotted the inscriptions engraved on the wall.

"I can't decipher them," Dr. Wirth said. "But you can, can't you, Dr. James? It's Greek, isn't it?"

Morgan stared at the markings. From what she could tell, the carvings appeared to be a strange mix of different languages. She could identify Greek symbols, but that was it. She sucked in an anxious breath.

Zach didn't take his gaze off the inscriptions. "I need something to write on."

One of the guards shoved a notepad and pen at him. He started scribbling. "It's not just Greek. There is Thai mixed in there, and Indonesian, too. Phaulkon was fluent in them all, and was known for his own form of note-taking."

"What's it say?" The woman pressed closer.

Morgan was tempted to smash her nose in.

"There." Zach held the pad out triumphantly. "This message was carved by a man named Luang Sri Wisan."

"Who was he?" Morgan asked.

Wirth smiled smugly. "He was one of the

deputies to the Siamese ambassador aboard the *Soleil d'Orient.*"

Zach nodded. "It also appears he was given a secret mission by Phaulkon. His job was to protect the amulet and hand it over to the King of France."

"Phaulkon was a fool to send it away," Wirth said.

"We may never know why he sent it away, but it says here that Luang Sri Wisan was found by locals who recognized the stone in the amulet." Zach's brow creased.

Morgan frowned. "Why would Malagasy locals recognize a stone in an amulet from Indonesia that was carried by a Siamese man?"

"They said it had to be returned to the Temple of the Ancients," Zach said slowly.

"Ancients?" Morgan prompted.

"Perhaps the Vizimba," Zach suggested. "The Malagasy believe the Vizimba were the first inhabitants of Madagascar. But legends about them vary from region to region. Some say they were smaller in stature, others say they were pale-skinned, and others say dark-skinned. Some even believe they were supernatural monsters."

"Oh, there were people here before the Vizimba," Wirth said with another smile. "Where does it say the Temple of the Ancients is?" Eagerness was stamped all over her face.

Zach stared at his notes. "It says it's north. In the forest of stone."

Morgan frowned. What the hell did that mean? She tried to sneak a look out of the cave. *Come on,*

Dec. She looked back and her gaze snagged with Zach's.

For a second, they stared at each other and Morgan quickly looked away. She'd known better than to be taken in by a charming adventurer. She knew she was an acquired taste. She didn't have a string of degrees or a smooth, charming manner. Her chest tightened and she fought to wrestle her unruly emotions under control.

Wirth smiled. She should have looked evil, but the big smile just made her look pretty. She could be anyone's cute sister or best friend. "I know exactly where the forest of stone is." She spun and stalked out of the cave. She waved a hand. "Bring them."

Chapter Fourteen

Zach was shoved roughly into the backseat of a mud-splattered jeep. Morgan was pushed in beside him, and the door was slammed closed.

"Are you okay?" He reached out to touch her.

She slapped his hand away. "What do you care? I'm just the hired muscle."

"Morgan—"

A guard slid into the driver's seat, and Wirth climbed into the passenger seat. Zach clamped down on the words he wanted to say. Surely Morgan hadn't bought his little act with Wirth? He'd been desperate to protect her and find a way to stop Wirth from killing her.

But as he stared at Morgan's set, blank face, he realized he'd maybe been a little too good with his act.

He closed his eyes for a second. He remembered what Hale had told him, and what he'd learned about Morgan Kincaid. She rarely let anyone in, and was quick to protect herself. She was sitting beside him, but was busy building up the defenses between them.

Panic flared. And there wasn't a fucking thing he could do about it right now.

The other guards climbed in behind Morgan and Zach, and slammed the doors closed. Outside, the heavens had really opened up, and the rain was pelting down. He looked out toward the sea, but could only see a wall of gray. No sign of the *Storm Nymph*.

Soon, they were headed down a bumpy dirt track. No one spoke, and before long, they turned onto a paved road.

The best Zach could tell, they were heading toward Tolagnaro.

He had so many questions, but he didn't dare ask anything. The tension in the vehicle didn't encourage friendly chitchat. He glanced out the window again. They would have been missed by now. Declan and the others would be searching for them.

Zach's mind turned to the incredible inscription they'd found. He couldn't believe that Luang Sri Wisan had been carrying the amulet, and had survived.

But what the hell was this Temple of the Ancients? None of it made sense.

When they reached the turnoff into Tolagnaro, they drove straight past it. Zach glanced at Morgan, but she stared ahead, ignoring him. He saw the way she was watching their captors intently. She'd be waiting for the right moment to attempt an escape.

Suddenly, he recognized exactly where they were going.

The airport.

They were waved through a gate, and drove right out onto the tarmac. They pulled up in front of a sleek, black helicopter.

Shit. This was not good. How would Declan ever find them?

Paris Wirth exited the vehicle, striding toward the aircraft. A pilot jumped out, and they had a short conversation. The pilot reached into the back of the helicopter and handed Wirth something.

Soon she was back, carrying a stack of clothes and boots. She tossed them on the seat between Morgan and Zach. "Change."

She turned and strode off.

The guards got out and stood outside the vehicle, and part turned away, offering Morgan and Zach the illusion of privacy.

"Morgan—"

"Just get changed, Zach."

"Morgan." He gripped her shoulders, forcing her to face him. "Listen to me—"

She jerked away, but he was determined to make her listen. He pushed her back against the seat and she wrenched as far away as she could. She got an arm free and slammed a fist against his jaw.

"Dammit." He ignored the pain. With a growl, he grabbed her, pulling her up against his chest. He sank one hand into her hair. "She was going to fucking shoot you. I would have said anything to protect you."

Morgan went still, her gaze raking his face.

He brushed his thumb over her cheek. "It was

all an act, Morgan. You are still the most fascinating, vital, and strongest woman I know."

Her eyelashes fluttered. "You lie well."

He tasted bile. "I learned early. It helped me avoid my father's beatings. Sometimes."

"I don't know what to believe."

"Believe in me."

"Zach, I'm not book smart, or elegant, or cultured—"

"Screw that, Morgan. You know what I came from. You think that really matters to me?"

"What you said...what you did..." She shook her head.

He'd hurt her. He realized now just how soft she was beneath her armor. "It was the only way I could think to protect you."

"Oh, Zach."

He leaned forward, his mouth touching hers. "I promised not to lie to you." His lips slid to her ear, nibbling at her lobe. "I want you, Morgan. More than I've ever wanted anything."

Her mouth met his in a quick, desperate kiss. "I'm sorry I didn't trust you."

"Hey, enough of that. Right now we need to stick together and find a way out of this situation."

She nodded. "We'd better get changed before they drag us out of here."

Zach started peeling off his damp wet suit, leaving his chest bare. Beside him, Morgan started doing the same thing.

"Just my luck that I get you half naked, and we're stuck in this situation," he grumbled.

She shimmied out of her wet suit, sitting on the seat beside him with her sleek, long legs and that tiny black bikini. She shot him a small smile.

He shoved the wet suit off and pulled on some cargo shorts. "If they fly us somewhere, how the hell will Declan find us?"

She motioned discreetly to the chunky watch on her wrist, and pitched her voice lower. "This has a tracker in it. Dec knows exactly where we are."

"I could kiss you right now," Zach said. "With lots of tongue."

A laugh burst out of her. "Only you could get me laughing while we're being held hostage by a dangerous group of black-market thieves."

"I wish we were somewhere else." His gaze drifted down her legs. "Just the two of us."

She cupped his cheek. "Don't worry, Dr. James. I'll get us out of here."

"Super-Morgan to the rescue."

She yanked a T-shirt over her head. "Sometimes I am pretty super, in fact. Whatever happens, just follow my lead." Then her face turned serious. "And do not *ever* throw yourself in front of a gun for me again."

Zach pulled a shirt on, doing up the buttons. Then he reached out and yanked her in for a fast and furious kiss. "I can be super as well, sometimes, and I don't want you injured. So, don't get hurt, understand? I've plans for this." He ran his hand down her body.

"I'm the security agent here, not you." But a tiny smile tugged at her lips.

"I see that smile."

"What smile?" She touched his face again. "And I have plans for you, too."

A fist pounded on the window, making both of them jump. They pulled their boots on. Zach's were a little large, but with the thick socks, they were fine. When they climbed out of the vehicle, the guards roughly bound their wrists and they were led to the helicopter.

Wirth met them. "You won't be needing this." The woman viciously wrenched Morgan's watch off her wrist and tossed it on the ground, before bringing her boot down on the timepiece, crushing it to pieces.

Morgan didn't react, but Zach knew she must be feeling the same gut-wrenching despair that he was. The two of them were shoved inside the helicopter, and into seats in the back.

Wirth climbed into the seat beside the pilot, and pulled a headset over her blonde hair. One of the guards slammed the door closed, and seconds later, the engines started, the rotors beginning to turn.

Zach scowled at the back of Wirth's head. Silk Road was crazy to think that they could do this. They blindly killed, kidnapped, and maimed, all in the pursuit of artifacts they could sell for top dollar.

The chopper rose and he looked outside. Hidden under his anger was a faint trace of excitement. The man in him was incensed, but the archeologist was excited. They were on the trail of the Phaulkon amulet, and a mysterious temple. Archeologists only ever dreamed of expeditions like this.

He could do without the thieves and killers, though.

As they traveled north, he watched the landscape below them change. The tropical green of the coast soon gave way to an arid, red landscape dotted with Madagascar's famous spiny forests. Soon, he saw evidence of the country's massive slash-and-burn deforestation. The local people were clearing away the forest at an incredible rate, causing terrible erosion and silting of rivers.

But he didn't have long to stare at the destruction as they continued onward, and the desert gave way to stony massifs and grasslands. He knew that there was some megalithic construction in the highlands—dolmens and standing stones. They were believed not to be very old, but could they form part of the Temple of the Ancients?

After a while, Wirth turned back to face them. "This is very exciting for me. I'm following in my renowned ancestor's footsteps."

Zach and Morgan stayed silent, but that didn't appear to bother Wirth.

"I'm related to Herman Wirth. He was an original founder of the Ahnenerbe," she said proudly.

Zach's blood went cold. "The Nazi archeological group tasked with proving the Aryan race was real, and that Germans were descended from them."

"They were pioneers, and ahead of their time," Wirth said, her eyes lighting. "They sent expeditions all around the world, searching for artifacts left by the master race."

"They were *Nazis*," Morgan said.

Wirth waved a dismissive hand. "Hunting for artifacts is in my blood. Did you know that my ancestor led a mission here to Madagascar?" She smiled, leaning toward them. "He went into the forest of stone and he came out with a Yaktavian bell."

"A what?" Morgan asked.

Zach stiffened. "Yaktavian bells are a crazy, unproven Nazi theory. There's no proof—"

Wirth slapped her hand against the seat. "Proof is *exactly* what Herman Wirth found here." Her voice rose. "He found a bell."

Zach sighed. This woman was a zealot. No amount of real evidence or facts would convince her otherwise.

"Okay, I'll ride this derailed train," Morgan said. "What is this bell?"

"The name Yaktavian is the name the members of the Ahnenerbe used for an advanced race they believed was destroyed by a flood," Zach said. "Others use the terms Atlanteans, Lemurians, take your pick. Of course, the Ahnenerbe had to invent their own name."

"The Ahnenerbe led expeditions all around the globe," Wirth insisted. "They were privy to information that none of us have ever seen. It was unfortunately all destroyed during the war."

Morgan nodded. "They should have thought of that before they committed genocide and, you know, invaded other countries."

A sour look crossed the woman's face.

"Unfortunately, the Ahnenerbe were also very good at mixing up facts, cherry picking what worked for their agenda, or just inventing 'facts' of their own," Zach said.

Wirth's face turned Arctic. "I thought you were smarter than this, Dr. James. I think I overestimated you."

He reached out and grabbed Morgan's hand. "I'm okay with that."

The woman's gaze lingered on their joined hands and then she sniffed. "Watch your words, both of you. Like I said, the Ahnenerbe were pioneers, and Herman found a bell here in Madagascar. Perhaps at the very temple we're searching for."

"So, what did these bells supposedly do?" Morgan asked. "Turn iron to gold? Water to wine?"

"The bells were resonant technology. They could be used as a means of protection, and also to move large stones and carve out tunnels." A wistful smile crossed her face. "I would give anything to find one. But for now, my focus is on the amulet and the powers of persuasion it possesses." A hungry look crossed the woman's face, and she nodded toward the window. "Ah, good. We're here."

The helicopter dipped, and out the window, Zach saw an amazing sight. Stretching as far as he could see, gray needles of rock pointed into the sky. A forest of stone.

Morgan leaned against him to get a better view, and gasped.

"Welcome to the Tsingy de Bemaraha Nature

Reserve." Wirth nodded to the pilot. "Take us down."

***

"There!" Hale pointed through the driving rain. "I can see a DPD."

Dec changed the direction of their inflatable boat. They raced toward the shore. Hale got a better view of the diving propulsion device resting on the sand. He'd used heavy-duty, military-grade ones when he'd been a SEAL. This one was a lighter, recreational model.

Whoever had snatched Morgan and Zach had used it to bring them ashore. He scanned the beach, but there was no sign of anyone on the empty shore.

The boat nudged the sand and Hale jumped out and pulled it farther from the water. He and Dec both pulled their weapons. Coop had drawn the short straw and had to stay on watch aboard the *Nymph*. They moved closer to the cliffs, searching for any hint that anyone had passed this way. The rain wasn't helping.

Hale kept his worry and anger suppressed. He'd had plenty of practice as a SEAL. Morgan was a hell of a fighter and he knew she wouldn't have let herself or Zach be taken easily.

She was either incapacitated or dead.

A muscle ticked in Hale's jaw. *Hell, no.* Morgan would do whatever she had to do to stay alive, and the way she and the archeologist were going, she'd do whatever she had to in order to keep the man safe.

Hale spotted something in the sand near the mouth of a cave. "There." He rushed over and crouched. There were several footprints in the sand.

He eyed them all. There were four sets of prints in dive boots, and one was smaller and slimmer than the others.

"They were here." He eyed the prints left by regular boots. "Two other men and a woman were here as well."

"Anything else?"

"Two bodies were lying on the ground over here." Hale pointed. "There are signs of a scuffle."

"Hope Morgan got some good hits in," Dec said darkly.

Hale released a breath. "All seven people walked out of here."

"Track them."

Hale set off, following the prints. Once they stepped off the sand, the trail was harder to follow, but he tracked the fine scrapes and crushed grass until he saw a set of tire tracks.

His hand curled into a fist. "They got into a vehicle." He stared at the wall of gray rain. Where the hell were they going?

Dec cursed. "Fucking Silk Road."

"If she can find a way to escape, Morgan will get Zach out," Hale said. "She'll protect him."

"That's what I'm afraid of." Dec swiped a hand through his sodden hair. "You've seen them together. She's falling for the guy...and I know Morgan. She'll protect him with her life."

Dec was right. Hale knew Morgan was tough and loyal. She wouldn't let anyone lay a hand on Zach James. Even if she got herself killed. "We need to find them."

His boss nodded and yanked out his phone. "I'm calling in Cal." Then Dec stared at his phone, his gaze narrowing. "And I have a message from Darcy." A sharp smile crossed his face. "It appears that two of our students have had large sums of money deposited in their bank accounts lately."

"Who?" Hale demanded.

"Charity and Max." Dec jerked a head back toward their boat. "Time to have a little friendly chat with them."

As they headed back to the boat, Hale glanced once more at the footprints that were slowly being washed away by the rain.

He and Morgan had been good friends from the day he'd joined THS. Like recognized like. They'd never shared their pasts, but he knew she had shadows she preferred not to discuss, and Hale had his own demons that were best kept locked away. Morgan had always respected that.

Hold on, Morgan. We'll find you.

***

Morgan didn't appreciate the handgun jammed into her back.

They'd landed on a flat patch of ground, and

were heading toward the stone forest. She could see narrow valleys between the rock formations, filled with trees and other vegetation. She also noted they only had a few more hours before sunset. At least her hands were free. One of the guards had cut their ropes off.

She glanced at the sky. How were Dec, Coop, and Hale going to find them?

"All this rock is easily soluble limestone," Wirth said from behind them in a chirpy tone, as though she were leading a tour group. "The *tsingy* rock formations were formed when water eroded the rock, and created this dramatic forest of needles. The groundwater has also gouged out a number of caves and caverns below."

Zach walked beside Morgan, staring up at the rocks with interest.

"Hey, don't look so happy," she muttered.

He schooled his features. "Sorry."

Damn archeologists. She stared up at the sharp peaks. She bet that Callum would give anything to climb here. The guy had rock climbing in the blood. Although, since he'd met photographer Dani, he didn't climb as much as he used to.

"The word tsingy comes from the local language and means 'place where one cannot walk barefoot'." Wirth smiled happily. "Be very careful not to fall on the rocks. They are very sharp, and can do a lot of damage."

Nice. "How can we possibly find anything in here?" Morgan said.

"We will," Wirth replied cheerily. "I have a rough

idea of the location of my ancestor's expedition. That's where we will begin looking."

They walked into a valley between the looming rocks. The stone was gray and rough-looking, and it didn't take long for the ground to turn rugged.

Morgan focused on climbing over rocks and up steeper parts of the path. The place was like a maze, and they hiked carefully through the twists and turns of the stone forest.

In some places, the rocks were wide apart, trees growing upward. In other parts, the rocks were close together, forcing them all to move in single file to slide through.

The shadows deepened. Wirth was looking at a tablet and checking GPS coordinates.

Moments later, they stepped out of a narrow pathway, and a giant chasm lay ahead of them. More tsingy rose up on the other side.

"Wow," Zach murmured.

Off to the left was a narrow rope bridge, spanning the gorge.

"Good. The expedition site is close." Wirth gestured Morgan onto the bridge. "Why don't you test out the strength of the bridge, Miss Kincaid?"

Bitch. Morgan stepped forward.

"I'll go." Zach pushed forward.

Morgan shook her head. "It's fine, Zach. Not my first rope bridge."

"Stay where you are, Dr. James," Wirth said, her tone less friendly now. Her demeanor toward Zach had cooled substantially.

Morgan stepped onto the narrow wooden planks,

gripping the ropes. The bridge looked to be in good condition. She walked slowly and cautiously forward.

When she reached the other side, she let out a relieved breath. She turned and watched, as the rest of the team started across.

"Are you okay?" Zach asked, when he reached the other side. His worried gaze locked with hers.

She nodded, warmth blooming in her chest. She wasn't used to someone worrying about her.

Wirth strode forward. "We're almost there."

They moved back into the tsingy. When they stepped out into a small clearing, Wirth stopped.

"This is the location of the Ahnenerbe expedition. Get to work, Dr. James. From the notes I've found, the archeologists back then found inscriptions on the rocks. I now believe they relate to the Phaulkon amulet."

Right. Morgan stared at all the rock around them. They were looking for a needle in a haystack.

They all fanned out, searching along the rock surfaces. Hell, even if something was here, it may have been worn off over time.

They spent an hour studying the rocks before they stopped for a rest. They were rapidly losing the light now. A water bottle was shoved at Morgan, and she and Zach both took sips.

"One more search before the sun sets," Wirth ordered.

Again, they moved back to searching the rocks. Morgan crouched down, pushing scraggly bushes out of the way. Nothing but rough stone.

Suddenly, Zach shouted, "Over here!"

Morgan hurried over, but Wirth beat her by a second. Zach was down on one knee, pointing to the rock.

The inscriptions were clearly visible. Morgan instantly made out the Thai and Greek letters.

"What do they say?" Wirth asked.

"They're a little bit worn." Zach ran his hands over the indentations. "But it says to head west for two *sen*, and look for more markings."

"Sen?" Wirth asked.

"An old Thai measurement. It's about forty meters."

The Silk Road guards flicked on flashlights. Wirth led them deeper into the forest of stone.

Zach kept his gaze on the rocks, and Morgan kept her gaze on him. Despite their circumstances, she enjoyed watching him work.

It really was getting too dark, but at the right distance, they fanned out again to study the rocks.

"Here," a guard called out.

Zach translated the inscription. East, one *sen*. They passed through a narrow passage of rock, and had to climb down a small cliff face.

Morgan leaped to the bottom, Zach right behind her. He touched the small of her back lightly, and Morgan decided if she was going to get kidnapped by psychopaths again, she wanted Zach with her.

The rocks gave way to another open space, and above, Morgan saw stars appearing in the sky. The hot day had given way to a warm night.

At the next location, they all used flashlights to

search the walls.

Nothing.

Not a single scratch.

Zach looked frustrated. "The light's not good enough. I don't know if I'm just missing it, or if it isn't even here."

Wirth moved, and before Morgan realized what the woman had planned, she pressed her gun to Morgan's head. Morgan forced herself to stay still, even though she wanted to turn and take the woman down.

But she couldn't risk Zach.

Zach held a hand up, his mouth a flat line. "That isn't necessary. I'll find it."

Chapter Fifteen

Morgan watched Zach as he got down on his knees. He held up a hand. "I need a flashlight."

One of the guards handed him one. He aimed it at the boulder, moving slowly along the wall.

Then he stilled, moving back a bit and shining the light at the base of the rock. Zach used his free hand to dig away some of the dirt.

He looked back at Morgan and grinned. "Found it! It's really worn, and was covered by debris."

He took a few moments to translate. "South-west. Three *sen*."

Morgan could watch him work for hours. It had taken her a little while, but she now realized the charming adventurer was just a façade. She liked the more serious nerd beneath. And she wanted to get him out of here.

Dec would have found her tracker at the airport. He had to have tracked their flight out of Tolagnaro, but she doubted Silk Road had filed an accurate flight plan.

But her team was coming. She was sure of it.

"It's too dark to continue," Wirth finally conceded. "We'll make camp."

The guards slipped off the backpacks they

carried, and Morgan and Zach were shoved down together on some rocks. One of the guards tossed them a couple of ready-to-eat meals, and a water bottle.

"Chicken teriyaki or beef, bean and rice burrito?" Morgan asked.

Zach winced. "I hate MREs. I'll take the chicken."

They ate quietly as Wirth's guards set up a tent for her. She sat inside, her face illuminated by her tablet. She was absorbed in whatever the hell she was looking at.

"We need to get away," Morgan whispered. "As soon as you stop being useful, we're both dead."

Zach took a drink of water. "Even if we get away, where the hell will we go? This place is very isolated." He closed the cap on the water bottle. "That's if getting out of the tsingy in the dark doesn't kill us, first."

"We'll worry about that after. For now, let's get away from Silk Road, and hole up somewhere for the night."

Two guards stayed close to Morgan and Zach, while the other two settled near Wirth's tent, curling up in sleeping bags.

Morgan stayed relaxed and alert. They just had to wait for the right moment. "Pretend to sleep."

Zach nodded, leaning back against the rock wall, and closing his eyes. Morgan did the same, but kept her eyes half open.

It took a while, but slowly, she watched the guards relax. They weren't expecting any trouble.

She glanced over and saw Wirth's tent was dark, and the other guards were deeply asleep.

Slowly, she reached out and tapped Zach's thigh. He nodded.

Morgan grabbed one of the large, loose rocks on the ground. She'd give anything for her SIG right now, or one of her knives.

She waited until both the guards on watch looked the other way, then she leaped up.

One swing and she slammed the rock into the closest guard's temple. He collapsed with a grunt. She caught his body and lowered him to the ground. It happened fast, but the other guard was already leaping up, fumbling to draw his gun from his holster.

Before Morgan could react, Zach charged forward. He slammed a punch into the guard's gut and he doubled over.

The man opened his mouth to shout. Morgan knocked Zach out of the way and wrapped her arm around the man's neck. He struggled, but she had a good grip. She held on tight, listening to the muffled choking noises. Finally, he slumped against her, unconscious.

She lowered his body down to the ground, then grabbed his decent Smith and Wesson. She rifled through his pockets.

"Remind me not to piss you off," Zach whispered.

Morgan glanced up and saw he'd grabbed a backpack and was shoving food, water and a sleeping bag into it. She looked over at Wirth's tent. No one appeared to have heard anything.

They needed to go. Now.

Morgan grabbed a flashlight and tossed a second at Zach. She kept the gun in her hand. "Let's go."

They headed back into the rocks, moving quietly. She tore a strip of fabric off her shirt and then pulled it over the flashlight. When she turned it on, it gave enough light to help them navigate, but hopefully wouldn't give their location away.

"How do you know where to go?" Zach asked.

"I memorized our way in."

"You *memorized* it?"

She shrugged. "I have a good memory."

"It all looks the same."

"There are always unique landmarks, if you take the time to find them."

They kept walking, but it wasn't long before she heard shouts and the sounds of pursuit behind them.

She lifted her gun. "Faster, Zach."

She grabbed his hand. Where the ground was flatter, they jogged. Where it was tougher going, they moved as fast as they could.

They reached the rope bridge, and quickly moved across it. On the other side, they kept moving through the maze of rocks.

Suddenly, they stepped out of the rocks and into a large, grassy valley. She saw another patch of tsingy ahead, but for now, they were free of the rocks.

To the north, the dark silhouette of the helicopter sat.

To the south, she saw trees.

She pointed. "That way. We need to get into the trees."

Together, they ran through the knee-high grass. By the time they reached the trees, they were both panting. Morgan's shirt was drenched in sweat. She glanced over at Zach and saw his hair was damp and pressed against his head.

Zach stopped, pressing his palms to his thighs, heaving in air.

"You keep going or we die," she told him.

He gave her a nod, and they set off again.

Finally, Morgan decided they'd put enough distance between them and Silk Road. "I think this is okay. They won't know which direction we headed. We need to find some shelter, and get some rest."

Zach groaned. "Everything hurts."

"Come on." She shone the flashlight around. They needed a place to sleep. As she moved the flashlight again, she stopped abruptly.

There was a large, roughly circular hole in front of them, and the beam glinted off something.

She gasped and realized they were standing on the edge of a large hole, with a pool of water at the bottom. The pool had a bank on one side, and trees and vines grew down to the water a few feet down.

Morgan knelt and shone the light in the hole. They stood on a natural overhang. She weighed the pros and cons. The overhang gave decent shelter, and they could wash in the water. No one would expect them to be hiding down there. But on the other hand, if they were discovered, they'd be trapped.

They were exhausted and needed to rest. They'd started their day hundreds of miles away on a ship, spent time scuba-diving, and escaped from thieving killers.

"We need to climb down there," she told Zach.

He groaned.

"Where's your famed sense of adventure?" she asked.

"I lost it about two miles back."

They found a place where they could use the brown, mangrove-like vines to climb down. Morgan dropped into a crouch beside the pool of water.

"We can set up the sleeping bag there." She pointed under the overhang.

Zach moved over and dropped the backpack. He grinned at her in the moonlight. "We made it."

"Yes, we did. Now we just need to get some rest, lay low, and wait for Declan to find us." Morgan set her gun and the rest of her gear down. "How about a swim?"

"Sounds like heaven. I'm sweaty as hell. If you can materialize a soft bed, too, I'd be a happy man."

Now that they were safe for the moment, Morgan felt something curling through her.

She yanked her shirt off, then unhooked her trousers and stepped out of them. Taking a deep breath, she slipped her bikini off. She looked over and saw Zach's eyes were wide and glued to her.

"I don't have a soft bed. Sorry to disappoint you, Dr. James."

"Disappoint me?" There was fire in his eyes and he started peeling off his shirt. "I'm definitely not disappointed."

***

Zach stripped off his sweaty clothes as fast as he could.

He watched Morgan wade out into the water. She looked like some warrior goddess, ready to take on the world. She was all sleek, long lines. Her strength was obvious, but it was mixed with a feminine sexiness he found irresistible. He wanted her more than he'd wanted any woman before.

She ducked down into the water and came back up, water streaming off her hair.

Zach followed her in, the water quite cool but not frigid. He stopped to scoop up some water and wash himself off. It felt so good to feel the cool water slick over his skin and wash him clean.

She swam over to him, low in the water. "You did good work today, and kept a cool head."

"You too."

She reared up and pressed her sleek, wet body against his. The clean, sexy, and dangerous scent of her swamped him. His cock was throbbing hard, and he knew she could hardly miss it, pressed against her belly.

Her hands tangled roughly in his hair. "You're pretty good in a fight."

"Coming from you, I suspect that's high praise." He ran his hands down her sides. He wanted to learn every part of her, find every sensitive spot.

She made a frustrated sound and yanked him forward. The kiss was rough, urgent, and needy. He cupped her ass, a deep sound vibrating in his throat. She was like a drug, and he couldn't get enough.

Zach needed Morgan. He wanted to sink inside her body, not only to prove they were still alive, but to claim her as his.

He slid one hand down her belly, teasing the curls at the juncture. "Spread your legs for me, Morgan."

She smiled up at him. "Make me."

"Always have to do everything the hard way." He leaned down and sank his teeth into the tendon in her neck.

With a wild sound, she arched into him. And when he nudged her legs apart, she let him, without thinking. "Sneaky," she murmured.

He slid his hand through her folds. She was damp and warm, and he shoved two fingers inside her.

She made a choked sound, jerking against him.

"You like that, Morgan? Filled up and stretched by my fingers?"

"Yes." Her hips bumped forward, her voice husky.

"This is where I want to be." He kept thrusting inside her, his thumb rolling her clit. She cried out, her strong body trembling. For him. "Where I belong."

"Zach." A husky cry.

"I want to come inside you, Morgan." Zach felt the hottest edge of frustration as he pulled his hand away. "I haven't been tested for a while, but on my last test I was healthy and I've always used protection. I, uh, don't have any condoms with me."

"I'm clean and I've had a contraceptive shot." Aqua-blue eyes stared up at him. She leaped up and wrapped her legs around his waist.

Zach took a step back, widening his stance, and cupped her butt. "Tonight, you're mine, Morgan."

"And you're mine, Zach."

His cock brushed against her, his gut tightening. "So damn wet."

"Get inside me. Now!"

The head of his cock parted her and she made a humming sound. Her hands bit into his biceps.

"Look at me," he growled.

She did, her eyes glittering with need. He thrust up, and at the same moment, she pushed her hips down. He felt her muscles stretch around him, felt her warmth.

"You're big," she gasped.

"You're perfect."

She moved up, sliding his cock out of her, then she slammed back down. His hands bit into the soft skin of her buttocks and he helped, jerking her body up and down on his. They found a rhythm, and Zach had to grit his teeth against the pleasure lashing at him.

Her rhythmic cries made him pump into her faster. Nothing had ever felt this good. He felt her muscles clenching on him, knew her release was rushing closer.

She threw her head back, her husky cries echoing around them. He felt himself trembling on the edge of a powerful orgasm.

He strode out of the water and back up onto the bank. In a few strides, he reached where he'd laid out the sleeping bag. He lay her down on it, gripped her hips and started hammering into her.

"More!" she cried, her nails scratching at his shoulders. One of her hands slid down and clamped on his ass, urging him on.

He needed more of her. Much more.

"I'm here, Zach. Take what you need. Take everything."

He kept thrusting into her, losing his smooth rhythm with the feel of her delicious body wrapped around him.

"Zach, yes, yes…"

She arched her back and cried out as she came, muffling the sound against his arm. The sound of his name, the feel of her, drove him into a frenzy. With another hard thrust, his release slammed into him. He groaned, spilling himself inside her milking warmth.

Chapter Sixteen

Morgan woke to warm lips moving across her belly.

She stretched, staring up at the night sky and the sprinkle of stars above. She knew exactly where she was, and exactly who was parting her thighs.

Zach's lips pressed against her inner thigh and she looked down at him. She wished they had more light, so she could see his face better.

After they'd fucked each other crazy, they'd fallen asleep. But it looked like the doctor was wide awake now.

His mouth pressed against the center of her, his tongue lapping at her. She bit her lip, her hips rearing up. "You're supposed to be resting," she gasped. "Restoring your energy."

His tongue circled her clit. "The sweet taste of you restores me. Listening to you moan does, too."

Incorrigible man. Then he got to work, licking and sucking. She locked her fingers in his hair, urging him on and letting him know exactly what she liked.

God. She was coming apart. She bit her lip, her back arching, her thighs clamping around his head.

A few more thrusts of that clever tongue and she

imploded. Pleasure swamped her and she thrust a fist to her mouth to stifle her scream.

But Morgan didn't drop back to rest. Oh, no. She needed more. She needed Zach inside her.

She sat up and tumbled him back onto the sleeping bag. She climbed up on top of him, and in the faint moonlight, she saw his wide smile. She gripped his hard cock, pumping it—once, twice. She traced a finger down one thick vein. It was a gorgeous cock—big and smooth.

Then, she lifted her hips. When the wide head bumped against her, he groaned. The sound made her smile, the heat in her growing.

She sank down on him. As she took the length of him inside her, he groaned again.

"Jesus," his voice was a rasp. "I need you so bad, Morgan."

She needed him, too. She started to ride him.

Morgan pressed her hands to his chest and threw her head back. Everything between her legs throbbed, and she loved feeling how much he stretched her.

"That's it." His hands were clamped on her hips, urging her on. "God, you're milking me hard."

She kept riding him, grinding down on his body. She leaned forward, changing the angle, pleasure arrowing through her, hot and searing.

"God, Morgan." His hands slid to her ass, taking handfuls of her cheeks as he worked her up and down on his cock. "Come for me."

She made a strangled sound. Her orgasm shimmered close, but just out of reach.

Then Zach reached between her legs and found her swollen clit. "Look at me."

She did. As he stroked her clit, as she thrust down on his cock, she couldn't look away from his face and the emotion she saw blazing in his eyes.

One more stroke and she flew apart. Zach reared up, his mouth taking hers as he swallowed her scream. His hands dug into her hips and he pressed her down and held her there, groaning as he found his own release.

Completely limp, she collapsed against him. He lowered them back down to the sleeping bag, keeping her on top of him. She wriggled to find a comfy spot on him. He stroked a hand down her back in lazy strokes, and she nuzzled her face into his neck.

Normally, if a man shared her bed, she liked to move to her side once they were done. She liked her space, and she'd never been good at sharing.

But she didn't want to move away from Zach.

She pressed a kiss to his warm skin, and when her eyelids felt heavy, she closed them. She'd just rest for a little while.

When she woke again, her back was cold. She glanced up and saw the stars were disappearing into a murky-lit sky. Dawn was coming.

She shivered, and instantly Zach moved. He rolled them to the side and shifted until he was pulling her closer. She nestled her back against his front. She was pretty sure she'd never spooned with anyone. She usually didn't like the feeling of someone at her back.

Heat poured off him, and it warmed her cool skin. A hard cock was also prodding her in the lower back.

"Nothing wrong with your stamina," she murmured.

His hand slid down over her hip, then gripped her thigh. He pulled it up, and the next second, he slid inside her from behind.

"Oh, God." She was swollen and sensitive, and it made him feel even bigger.

With slow, steady thrusts, Zach kept up the rhythm. His arms wrapped around her and she felt protected and cared for. It was almost sweet.

"Morgan." His teeth grazed her neck.

It was just sex. She said the words in her head, over and over. She couldn't get too attached to him. She stared blindly at the rock wall in front of her, as Zach's big cock stretched her, pushing her closer and closer to her ultimate pleasure. And then she came, her body shaking. A second later, he pushed inside her once more and held himself there, as he spilled inside her.

They lay together for a long moment, sated and pleasured. Morgan just kept staring at the rock wall. She'd never felt this connected to a man before. She wanted to touch him, kiss him, cuddle him, hear his laugh. God, Morgan *did not* cuddle.

Everything was fine. She knew their emotions were heightened by the dangerous situation. Besides, Zach was a man who traveled the globe looking for adventure. He didn't stay in one place, and he didn't stay with one woman.

But would he stay if he knew she was thinking she wanted more?

She kept staring at the wall, their little alcove brightening as the sun approached the horizon. There was...something...on the rock. Frowning, she studied it. Maybe she was imagining things?

But as the sky continued to lighten, she pulled away from Zach and sat up.

"What is it?" he asked.

"Where's the flashlight?"

He slapped it into her palm and she flicked it on. She aimed it at the rock wall.

Inscriptions. Just like the others they'd found in the tsingy.

"Holy Mother of God." Zach sat up and crawled closer. His lips moved, as his gaze flew back and forth over the inscription.

Morgan smiled to herself. Nothing like watching a sexy, naked man being all studious.

He looked back over his shoulder, glancing at the pool.

"The pool is covering a cave," he said.

She frowned, staring at the still water. "A flooded cave? Like the one you mentioned to me? Where the scientist discovered the giant lemur bones?"

He nodded, his eyes glowing. "But at the bottom of this cave is the Temple of the Ancients."

***

Zach couldn't believe it. That gentle pool of water

was hiding the temple and possibly the Phaulkon amulet.

Morgan's face was serious. "We have no way of knowing how large these caves are, and if there are any pockets of air down there."

He nodded. "Some of the caves the paleontologists dived were over a kilometer long."

"We'll need dive gear."

Zach's shoulders slumped. "I'll get right on that." The excitement he'd felt only seconds ago vanished.

She looked at him. "I saw dive gear on the helicopter."

Every thought flew out of his head. "What? You're talking about the helicopter owned by *Silk Road*."

"We can go back, sneak in, and take the equipment we need."

"Go back? Have you lost your mind?" He didn't want Morgan anywhere near Paris Wirth and her obsessive desire for the amulet.

"They won't be expecting us to go back," Morgan continued. "You want to find the temple, don't you? And the Phaulkon amulet?"

He thrust a hand through his hair. Of course, he wanted to find them. But more than that, he wanted Morgan safe. He didn't tell her that, though, because he knew that Morgan was more than capable of taking care of herself. If he told her that he wanted to protect her, she'd probably hit him.

"We should get out of here," he said. "Trek toward a town."

"You decoded the first few inscriptions," she said. "You don't think Wirth will be able to work out the rest on her own, now? They'll lead her right here." Morgan shook her head. "It's harsh, isolated terrain. Trekking out of here might kill us. And I am *not* letting that woman get the amulet. She's attacked us, hurt you and Diego. I'm not letting her win."

Zach thrust his hands on his hips and released a long breath. "I don't like this."

"I know. But our options are severely limited."

He stared at her, at that amazing strength that would intimidate so many people, but that he found insanely attractive. "Okay. Let's do it."

She grinned. "Excellent decision."

"Don't make me regret it."

They took a few minutes to get dressed and prepped. Morgan shoved her handgun in her pocket. Then they climbed out of their little sanctuary, and started the trek back toward the helicopter.

More of the surrounding tsingy formations were visible in the daylight. The trees weren't very high or thick, and just off to their left, he spotted a shallow river. Morgan moved like a ghost through the trees, silent and lethal.

An animal darted out in front of them. It was small and covered in white fur. Zach watched the lemur pause to look at them, lifting his long tail. While his body was all white, his face was black and dominated by round, yellow eyes.

As several more crossed to join their friend,

Morgan smiled. "Cute little guys."

Soon, they reached the edge of the sparse trees, and the helicopter was visible ahead. Morgan waved for him to get down and they crouched behind a tree. The trip back hadn't felt anywhere near as long as their escape run the night before.

They scanned their surroundings. Zach could only see the pilot, who looked like he was asleep in the cockpit of the chopper.

"No sign of Wirth and her guards." Morgan lifted her handgun. "Let's do this. Fast and quiet. I'll take care of the pilot, and you get in the back and get the dive gear."

Zach nodded. She moved fast, and he moved behind her, trying to move with the same stealth.

They slowed as they neared the helicopter, coming in from an angle where the pilot wouldn't see them.

Then Morgan sprang. She wrenched open the cockpit door, reached in, and yanked the pilot out. He fell into the dirt and opened his mouth to scream. Morgan hit him in the face with the butt of her gun. He dropped back on the ground, blinking. She hit him again, and he was out cold.

Damn. "Beautiful, smart, and efficient. And scary." Zach smiled at her. "You are incredible."

A flash of vulnerability crossed her face in the early morning light. "No one's ever thought so before."

"Then they were idiots."

She smiled now. "Save the flattery for later. Now move that fine butt of yours."

Zach opened the door of the helicopter, and climbed in.

"We need to make it quick," Morgan reminded him.

He went to the back of the aircraft and started pulling open storage cupboards. The dive gear was neatly stacked in one corner. It was all top-of-the-line, and he gave a low whistle. He handed it out to Morgan.

"Look at this stuff," he said. "Streamlined, lightweight tanks, and full-face masks with integrated communications."

"Pays to be a bad guy," she replied dryly. She set the gear down, checking the air in the tanks. "This is nice."

Zach also grabbed a backpack and stuffed anything useful that he could find—food, ammunition, first aid kit—inside. He leaped out of the helicopter, and they divvied up the gear.

"Let's go," he said.

Soon, they were jogging back into the trees. Zach half expected to hear shouts and the whistle of bullets whizzing past him.

But there was nothing but some birds calling in the quiet morning.

They'd made it. They grinned at each other as they headed back to the pool.

***

Morgan checked the tanks, and laid out all the dive gear beside the pool.

Like Zach had said, the gear was top-of-the-line. Nothing but the best for Silk Road. Her jaw tightened. The group really needed to be stopped, one way or another.

She glanced over at Zach, who was standing beside the pool, staring down at the water. He looked tense.

"You okay?" Her shoulder brushed against his.

"It could be dangerous down there."

"We'll take it slow." She gripped his arm. "And I'll take care of you, Dr. James."

There was something in his eyes. "Because it's your job?"

Her heart clenched. "That's part of it."

"What's the other part?"

Her mouth went dry.

"We're stuck in the middle of nowhere, Morgan. Silk Road people are somewhere nearby, hunting us and this treasure. Declan may or may not be able to find us, and we're about to dive in a dangerous, flooded cave. Tell me."

She tilted her head, her stomach tight. "I'm not good with words."

"So show me."

There was so much swirling in his eyes. She fisted her hands in his shirt, and yanked him closer. Their mouths fused, and she poured everything into the kiss. All the volatile emotions she felt for this man.

"Zach." One tortured word, torn from her.

"I know." His voice was deep and rough. "I have to have you."

He backed her up, under the overhang. She found herself spun around, and she pressed her hands against the rock wall to steady herself. His hands were at the waistband of her trousers, tearing them open. He shoved her trousers down, and then she heard the zipper of his shorts.

She knew they didn't have time for this, but as his hands moved over her bare ass, she also knew she needed it. More than anything.

The next thing she knew, the large head of his cock was prodding her, and he thrust inside.

She moaned, her palms flat against the rock. He thrust inside her, heavily.

"You'll feel me." His voice was a growl. "Even after I slide out of you, you'll know I was here."

He leaned forward, nipping her shoulder. She pushed back against him.

"This isn't just sex, Morgan. I belong here. I'm going to be inside you again. You're mine."

She was shoving back against him now, straining toward a fast, hard release. His fingers were biting into her hips, and he was powering inside her like he wanted to claim her. Electric fear skated through her. For the first time in her life, she wanted to be claimed.

"I've never wanted a woman the way I want you." His tone darkened. "I've never committed to a woman because I've been too afraid of the bad blood in my veins. Afraid I'd hurt her. But you...I can't stay away from you."

His hands slid down her belly, his thumb finding her slick clit. He rubbed it, and she flew apart. She bit her tongue to keep from crying out, and as pleasure cascaded through her, he groaned his own release.

With both of them spent, he pulled out of her, and she bit her lip, feeling his withdrawal. He turned her around, and pressed a lingering kiss to her lips. "There is going to be an 'us', Morgan. Just giving you some warning."

Her chest went tight. "You like adventures," she said. "You told me you love to travel, and dig, and dive. Not to be tied down."

"Well, I guess I'm ready for another kind of adventure," he said.

Warmth flooded her. She wanted to trust it and she wanted to trust him. "Um, I can strip down a gun and throw a knife dead on target. I know a dozen different ways to kill a man, but I'm really bad at relationships."

His thumb brushed her wrist. "I'll go easy on you."

"I'll try to push you away, or I'll screw up. You'll get tired of me—"

"Hey, enough of that. I'm a patient man, and we'll learn together."

She remembered the dark words that had torn out of him earlier. "Zach, you've only mentioned a little about your father, but you aren't like him."

His jaw tightened. "I look like him. Every time I look in the mirror, I see him."

"You escaped. You've made something of yourself, while he beat up on a small boy he was supposed to protect."

Zach stayed tense and silent.

She tangled her fingers with his. "Maybe it's time to stop running and realize there's nothing to run from anymore."

Something moved through his gaze. "You going to stick around and help me with that?"

"Maybe I will." Morgan straightened. She glanced at the water and the dive gear. It was time to focus on the task at hand. "But right now, we have another adventure to deal with."

He scrounged up a smile, dimples winking. "You're talking about diving, right? Not another intense quickie?"

"Yes, diving, smart ass." She held out a wet suit for him. He pulled it on, and while he grabbed his BCD jacket and tanks, Morgan pulled her own gear on.

He settled his full-face mask over his face. "Testing. Can you hear me?"

His voice came through the speakers in her mask. "Loud and clear."

Flashlights were mounted on either side of the mask, and she flicked them on. Together, they waded into the pool.

Zach nodded. "Let's go find some treasure."

Chapter Seventeen

As they sank down into the water, Morgan looked at the rocks below them.

In some places, they looked round and curved, and in others, sharp and pointed, just like the tsingy. Beautiful rays of light speared into the water, but as they swam deeper, the blackness encroached.

Complete and unforgiving.

They descended farther, and now the only light came from the lights on their masks. Morgan had done some cave diving before. Even though it was interesting, she always preferred the open ocean and being surrounded by endless possibilities, not caged in by rock walls.

The cave narrowed, and became more horizontal. She saw the gap ahead narrowed, and was flanked by giant slabs of rock. Thankfully, they still had plenty of room to maneuver.

In places, she could see sandy patches dotting the rock floor. The cave widened again, and now, pillars of rock extended from the floor to the roof. As the light cut through the water, illuminating the colonnade, she got the feeling of being in an underwater church.

And then she spotted the bones.

Wow. Numerous brown-colored bones lay, partly buried in the gravelly bottom. Several large skulls lay on the sand, large, empty eye sockets staring upward, unseeing.

"It's amazing," she said.

"An ancient graveyard," Zach said, looking around. "These probably belong to long-extinct creatures."

Morgan lifted a skull, almost as big as her own. "Not sure I would have wanted to run into this guy."

"Must be from one of the giant lemurs."

She set it back down and they kept moving. Soon, the cave started to narrow again. Morgan swam first, Zach right behind her. She checked her air gauge. "If the cave goes much farther, we'll have to turn back, or we won't have enough air to get to the surface."

All of a sudden, Zach bit out a curse. Morgan spun and saw rocks falling from the roof. She kicked hard, knocking Zach out of the way.

A rock struck her shoulder, knocking her sideways. She bumped into the rock wall, and felt another rock hit her back, striking her tank.

Morgan tried to swim and realized she couldn't move. The rock had pinned her tank against the cave wall.

"I'm stuck," she said.

"Shit!" Zach appeared and reached past her, tugging at the rocks. He dropped back, floating in the water. "No luck. They won't budge.

He leaned forward again, attacking the large rock pinning her. It wouldn't move. He kept at it, and she could hear his fast breaths through her comm link. He was just wasting his oxygen.

"Zach. Stop."

He did, his face just inches from hers.

"Zach, you need to go."

"And leave you?" His eyes narrowed.

"Yes. It's the only—"

"Fuck that." His hands cupped either side of her mask. "Never."

Fear ate at her. Morgan rarely felt fear. From the day she'd lost her father, she'd learned to curb it, ignore it, control it. But now, she felt fear greater than anything she'd ever felt, because she knew Zach wouldn't leave her.

She had to convince him. "I don't want you to die down here."

She felt his fingers brush against her cheek. "Right back at you. I'm falling in love with you."

God. Morgan felt hot and cold, afraid and elated, all at once. "Zach—"

"So, screw your rules. When we get out of here, I'm going to hold your hand, carry your bags, take you on dates, and give you unlimited orgasms. I'm going to make you fall in love with me. Got it?"

She felt tears pricking at her eyes. She wanted that. So much.

But for now, she needed to keep the stubborn man alive.

With renewed focus, she turned the problem over in her head. "I'm going to slip out of my gear."

Now she saw concern in his eyes. "You can use my octopus."

The spare regulator attached to his BCD. "On your tanks alone, both of us breathing, we won't make it to the top. I'll hold my breath as long as I can and you pull me—"

He shook his head. "You're the stronger swimmer and better diver. You should pull me."

Her stomach did a slow roll. The thought of him drowning and her having to pull him behind her, lifeless, made her feel ill. The truth was, though, however they did it, they were unlikely to both make it to the surface.

And the stubborn fool wouldn't leave her.

"Or," he said. "We continue on." He waggled his eyebrows. "Want to live dangerously, Miss Kincaid?"

No, but it was better than staying stuck here. "I want to live."

He grabbed her hand. "Come on, Morgan. We're together and that's all that matters to me." He pressed his mask against hers. "I want to kiss you so badly."

She groaned. "That's good incentive. You can kiss me when we get to the other end."

Morgan took a deep breath, then disconnected her mask. She slipped free of her gear. Instantly, Zach pressed his second regulator to her mask, and she breathed deep.

They started swimming, kicking strongly, and moving as fast as they could, deeper into the cave.

They kept going and going. Finally, Zach's tank was showing empty.

She took another deep breath and disconnected from his tanks. She could hold her breath a long time and she kicked, single-mindedly moving ahead, praying for a miracle. An air pocket, a dry cavern, anything.

Her lungs started to burn, and beside her, she felt Zach jerk.

His air had run out.

She urged him to keep swimming, and saw he was struggling not to take a breath. He was losing strength, his movements uncoordinated. She grabbed the back of his wet suit and kept powering forward, dragging him behind her.

Come on. She couldn't believe that she could finally start falling in love with a man and then lose him.

Zach went limp. Despair screamed through her when she realized he'd drowned. *No!*

Morgan kept kicking. She couldn't bear to look at him. The burning in her lungs reached breaking point and her vision blurred, splotches of light dominating her vision.

They were out of time.

***

Zach felt lips on his.

He *knew* those lips. He lifted his head, sank a hand into her wet hair, and kissed Morgan hard.

She was wet, and his own skin was wet. He

nipped her lip. "Heaven is far wetter than I imagined."

"Thank God, Zach." She gave a watery laugh. "Are you okay?"

He opened his eyes. She was leaning over him, misery on her face. He cupped her cheek. "I'm okay."

She released a shaky breath. "I've been doing resuscitation for the last ten minutes." Her chest hitched. "I thought I'd lost you."

He sat up and pulled her into his lap. He slicked her wet hair back from her face and held on tight. She burrowed her head against his chest, and he felt her shaking.

God. He held on tight to his tough, strong woman, and knew he never wanted to let her go. Reluctantly, Zach lifted his head. He saw they were in a cavern, their legs still resting in water while they sat on a rocky shore. "We made it."

"I didn't think we were going to."

He pressed a soft kiss to her lips. "We made it, thanks to you."

She cupped his cheeks firmly. "Let's not do that again."

They stayed there, holding each other for several minutes. When they finally broke apart and stood, Zach's legs felt a little shaky. He watched Morgan pull out her gun and dewater it.

"Will that still work?" he asked. "Won't it backfire, or something, if you use it?"

She arched a brow at him. "It doesn't have gunpowder in it."

"Right."

She shook her head. "If we're going to, you know, be together, we'll have to bring your gun knowledge up to speed."

He grinned. "Yes, Miss Kincaid. And if I'm a naughty student, you'll have to discipline me."

A laugh broke out of her. "You nearly died a few minutes ago, and you're already thinking up lurid fantasies."

"Yep. Will you wear a tight pencil skirt and sexy glasses?"

She turned to face the tunnel ahead. "Focus, Dr. James."

Zach stared at the dark cave ahead, and that was when it dawned on him that they could see. The light wasn't great, but a pink glow lit the cave ahead. "Why can we see?"

"No idea. Let's find out."

They walked on, the rocks crunching under their feet. The walls of the cave were damp, and twinkled with a faint sparkle of light. It made Zach think of glitter.

"This reminds me of the underwater temple we found in Cambodia," Morgan said. "On a previous job."

"You were on that expedition?" Zach had read about Treasure Hunter Security discovering an ancient temple in the mountains around Angkor.

Morgan shivered. "Yes. There was also this giant snake."

"No dangerous snakes in Madagascar. And no giant ones that I know about."

"Good." Suddenly, she pulled him to a stop. "Jesus, look."

Zach turned his head. The cave opened up into a small cavern, and translucent pink stones were nestled inside, standing upright in a circular pattern.

They'd found the temple.

***

Morgan just stared at the massive stones looming ahead of them. The rocks gave off a faint glow.

It looked nothing like a Greek or Roman temple, with elegant columns and smooth walls. Or the intricate architecture of Angkor Wat in Cambodia.

This temple almost looked natural, like the Earth itself had set these rocks in place, in an era far older than time itself.

As they walked toward the structure, a feeling of peace and tranquility washed over Morgan. She frowned, her muscles relaxing of their own accord. The place exuded a quiet, calming energy.

"It almost looks natural," she said.

Zach nodded. "A lot of megalithic temples do. The prehistoric people carved into rocks, used natural stones. But this was definitely made by man."

She watched Zach's face as he walked around, touching the translucent stone. Wonder. Awe. The man was in his element, doing what he loved.

Then her chest tightened, flutters taking up residence in her belly. She realized that he looked at her exactly the same way.

She turned to stare blindly at the temple, trying to contain the big emotions inside her. Giant stones were balanced on other upright stones, like lintels on a doorway.

Zach smoothed his hand over one of the rocks. "This feels almost warm. It's amazing."

"The rock looks a bit like the uncut diamonds." She froze. Surely the temple wasn't made of diamond?

Zach scratched a nail against the rock. "It's not diamond, but I've never seen rock like it before."

She looked around again. "This place feels..."

"Peaceful?"

"Yeah."

They skirted some large rocks, heading toward the center of the space. There was a large, altar-like boulder, sitting in the very center.

And resting on top of it was a necklace.

They both froze, staring at it.

"Go on." She nudged Zach.

He moved forward and reached for the necklace. He lifted it in his hands, and turned back toward her. It had a sturdy metal chain that had been tarnished by time. The pendant itself was a circle, made of what looked like gold, but it wasn't tarnished at all. It looked like it had just been polished.

In the center of the pendant was a stone orb, made of the same milky-pink, translucent material as the temple around them.

"That was how the locals who found Luang Sri

Wisan knew the amulet belonged here," Zach said. He turned and grinned at her. "We found the Phaulkon amulet."

"Congratulations, Dr. James."

Sounds suddenly echoed around the cavern.

Morgan spun and lifted her gun. She heard the splash of water, and voices. Quickly, she waved Zach down and she ducked behind a massive stone.

She peered around it and saw Paris Wirth and her guards coming out of the water, all wearing dive gear.

Morgan ducked back. "Shit. It's Wirth. Somehow she found us."

Shots rang out, pinging off the large stones. She crawled over to Zach. "Keep your head down.

"I know you're in here, Miss Kincaid, Dr. James." Wirth's voice rang in the space. "Unfortunately for you, we have trackers in our diving equipment. We followed you right here...to this amazing temple."

Zach muttered a curse.

Morgan ground her teeth together. "I should have thought of that."

More bullets ricocheted off the rocks nearby.

"I want that amulet," Wirth called out.

Morgan popped up to take a shot. More bullets pinged, and she ducked back down.

Suddenly, Zach hissed out a breath. She turned, and saw a tear through his wet suit, on his bicep. There was blood.

He'd been shot. "Zach!"

He slapped a hand over it. "It's just a graze. I

can't even feel it."

Morgan looked around. Where could they go? Wirth and her team were blocking the way back to the water. And even if they could get there, they wouldn't have time to steal dive gear.

Morgan was well aware that now that Wirth had found the temple, the woman had no reason to keep them alive.

"Back." Morgan jabbed a finger toward the back of the temple. They scooted behind some other rocks, more gunfire sounding.

At the back of the cavern, behind the temple, there was an entrance to a tunnel in the rock. Her pulse spiked. "That could be a way out."

"Or a dead end," Zach said grimly.

They were edging toward the tunnel, when a strange noise rumbled out of the dark space. A deep-throated sound that made the hair on Morgan's arms rise.

They both froze, and stared into the darkness. What the hell was down there?

Chapter Eighteen

Zach stared into the tunnel. Shadows were moving around in there. Big shadows.

Bullets ricocheted off the wall nearby, and Morgan returned fire.

"There's something down there, Morgan."

"I know. But the Silk Road guards are getting closer, Zach. We need to get out of here."

"I think going down there would be a very bad idea." They were caught between Silk Road, and whatever the hell was lurking in the darkness.

A volley of gunfire hit the wall above their heads. They both crouched low.

Zach caught a flash of movement from the tunnel. Something huge rushed out.

"Get down!" He tackled Morgan, rolling them out of the way.

Massive, dark shapes leaped over them.

Shocked screams filled the cavern. More gunfire and deep, explosive grunting noises, echoed deafeningly through the cavern. Then, there were thumping sounds, and some of the screams cut off.

"No!" Wirth's higher-pitched scream. "No, stop!"

Zach lifted his head to peer around the pillar and saw...creatures.

They were leaping over the temple stones with ease, and attacking the Silk Road people. They looked like gorillas. They had large, powerful bodies, and black-and-gray fur. When they moved, they thumped their giant hands, or paws, down. He watched in horror, as one animal swung its arm and hit a guard. The guard's body flew through the air, and smashed into a stone.

"Come on." He grabbed Morgan's hand, and pulled her away from the chaos. They moved right to the edge of the cavern, hiding in a pocket of darkness.

One of the giant creatures lifted up another guard, holding him high in the air. As the animal started to slam the screaming man down, Zach looked away.

Morgan was shaking her head, her eyes wide. "What the hell?"

"They're giant lemurs," Zach whispered.

Her eyes widened even more. "But they're extinct."

"Apparently not."

"These animals don't have tails, and they aren't cute and friendly."

"No."

"I thought lemurs were vegetarian," she said.

"I don't think they are killing for hunger. They're protecting their territory."

The screams and gunfire were becoming sporadic now, punctuated by the grunts of the animals. Zach glanced around. They needed a better place to hide. His gaze landed on the water.

"Morgan, we need to get into the water."

She nodded and they carefully edged along the wall. They moved agonizingly slowly, not wanting to catch the attention of any of the creatures.

Zach and Morgan reached the water and slid in as quickly and quietly as possible. They sank down, until just their eyes and noses were above the water.

They had a perfect view of the frenzy.

Another guard slammed into a rock, accompanied by the macabre sound of bones snapping. Zach closed his eyes for a second and told himself not to feel sorry for those Silk Road bastards.

But still, he wasn't sure anyone deserved a death like this.

The frenzy slowly died down. The creatures walked around, sniffing. All the Silk Road people had been dispatched. Zach could see Wirth's slim leg sticking out from behind a pillar. She was motionless.

Then Morgan nudged Zach, nodding her head toward their original hiding place. One of the giant lemurs was sniffing along the wall where they'd secreted themselves. It was making its way toward the water.

"Fuck." He tensed and grabbed Morgan's hand.

The creature stopped near the water's edge and lifted its gaze. It looked right at them, with large, yellow eyes.

It made some grunts and a chirping noise. The others crowded around it, all of them tense, energy pumping off them. All of them stared silently at Zach and Morgan in the water.

"I'll attack them," Morgan whispered. "You race through the temple and get to the tunnel at the back."

He didn't respond. He wasn't leaving her to face these creatures alone.

Slowly, the two of them rose above the surface, water streaming off their bodies.

Then the creatures tilted their heads and went still. Every pair of eyes was looking at Zach's pocket. He glanced down. No. Not his pocket; they were looking at the amulet.

One by one, he watched the giant, muscular bodies relax, their aggression disappearing. A few even sat down, staring quietly at them.

What the hell? Zach looked at Morgan, and then back at the now docile giant lemurs.

***

Zach held up the Phaulkon amulet, understanding lighting his eyes. "The amulet is soothing them."

Morgan had no idea how that was possible, but she lowered her gun. "All signs of aggression are gone."

They all stood there, frozen in a strange tableau. Then slowly, one by one, the lemurs started to withdraw. They crossed back through the temple, walking on all fours, and disappeared back into the tunnel.

Morgan released a breath. "God."

"That was close," Zach said.

Morgan moved over to check the Silk Road diving equipment resting near the water's edge. She cursed. "It's all damaged." She kicked a mangled tank. "It's useless. Dammit." Great, they were now stuck in an underground cave with killer lemurs.

"Maybe we should try the tunnel?" Zach said.

Her eyes widened. "The one with the killer animals lurking in it?"

He lifted the amulet. "We've got this."

"That's mine!" Paris Wirth lunged out from behind a standing stone.

Her clothes were torn and bloody. She was dragging one leg behind her, and holding a gun in a shaking hand.

She aimed the gun at Zach. "I want my amulet."

Morgan lifted her own weapon, holding it tightly with both hands. "That's not going to happen."

"You shoot me, and I'll fire. Dr. James will die."

Morgan felt that familiar calm settle over her. Whenever she was on a mission, in combat, she felt a kind of peace and serenity that she rarely felt anywhere else. Her thoughts cleared, and her reflexes sharpened. This was what she did best.

She took a slow step forward. "I doubt that."

Wirth's hand tightened on her weapon. "I'll do it."

"Not with the safety on." Morgan fired.

The shot hit Wirth in the chest. Blood bloomed, soaking her shirt. With a shocked look on her face, the woman fell backward.

Morgan stepped forward and kicked the woman's weapon away.

Zach stepped up beside Morgan. "Have I told you how amazing you are? Especially when you're being all tough and badass?"

Warmth blossomed inside her. Zach really loved her for her. He saw all the parts of her that had scared so many people off in the past, and he liked them. "No."

He pulled her into his arms. "Well, you are."

She felt the amulet jab into her belly. She looked at it. "Well, you found the amulet. Not to mention an ancient temple."

"Yeah."

She tilted her head. "You don't sound very happy."

"I'm not sure it was worth all of this." He shook his head. "You know what? I couldn't care less about this thing." He shoved it into his pocket. "There's a treasure of a different kind that I want even more."

Morgan's throat went dry. Now this adventure was over, he was already thinking of the next one? Would he feel the same way about her, given enough time? Just like every other man she'd brushed up against.

Zach shook his head. "God, I can read every thought going through your head." He shot her a smile. "I want *you*, Morgan."

"Really?"

"I want to take you on a third date."

She frowned. "Huh?"

"Hale told me all about how you only have first dates, and rarely let a man have a second one. So, we'll skip one and two, and just go right on to number three. Three's my lucky number, you know?"

She smiled at his handsome face. "What would this third date look like?"

"We'll have it at the museum. It's got this rooftop terrace that looks back over the city skyline. I'll set up a table for two, we'll have cocktails. I know you'd prefer beer, but you need to try new things sometimes, too. To eat, something chocolate. Maybe chocolate fondue."

He *knew* her. Tears threatened and she fought them back. Not since her father had died had anyone truly known her.

"I want that." She stepped close, pressing her hand to his chest. "I want you."

"What do those rules of yours say about saying 'I love you'?"

God. "Zach—" she could barely get the words out as she cupped his cheek "—let's find a way out of here, and then you can tell me."

***

Zach watched an agitated Morgan stride around the cave for the tenth time. Frustration was coming off her in waves.

"There has to be *some* way out," she snapped.

They both knew they'd never make the swim without tanks. And they'd even explored the lemur tunnel at the back. Unfortunately, it had narrowed to nothing.

They had no idea where the creatures had vanished to.

So, Morgan and Zach were trapped.

Finally, she spun to him, her hands on her hips. "I'll dive out. I'm the best swimmer."

He scowled at her. "It's too far. You'll never make it, Morgan. I'm not going to let you die."

She stepped up to him, toe to toe. "And I won't let you die here."

He gripped her shoulders. "You aren't swimming—"

"You two still arguing?"

Declan Ward's deep voice made them both spin.

Dec, flanked by Hale and Ronin, along with another man who looked like a slightly-less-rugged version of Declan were coming up above the water, all of them dressed in dive gear.

Morgan broke into a wide smile. "We are damn happy to see you guys! How did you find us?"

"Well, we found out a Silk Road helicopter had left Tolagnaro airport not long after you two went missing," Declan said. "I called Cal in to help, and while we waited for him to arrive, Darcy managed to track where the helicopter went. Cal arrived with a chopper of our own, and we followed you."

"How did you find the cave?" Zach asked.

"Oh, we had a *nice* chat with the Silk Road chopper pilot," Cal said. "He told us how to follow the signal from their diving gear."

Declan scanned the temple, taking in the dead

bodies. "You've been busy."

"It was the lemurs," Morgan said.

When Declan shot her an incredulous look, Zach waved a hand. "It's a long story."

"It really is," Morgan added.

Zach reached into his pocket and held up the amulet.

Declan nodded. "Well done, Zach. So, do you two want to finish your argument, or get out of here?"

"Let's go," Morgan said, leaning into Zach. "Please."

Zach found himself buddied up with Ronin, using his spare regulator. Morgan swam ahead with Hale. As they made their way back through the flooded cave, Zach was too tired to even look at the bones littering it.

Soon, he was climbing out of the pool where they'd spent the night. As he stood by the water's edge, his muscles protested, and fatigue threatened to swamp him.

"I just want to curl up in a soft bed," he said with a moan.

Morgan smiled at him, shaking the water out of her hair. "You'll get a bed soon enough." She looked away, looking a little nervous.

Morgan was never nervous.

Zach strode up to her, sweeping her into his arms. He felt her teammates stop what they were doing to watch.

"I love you, Morgan Kincaid. Every strong and fascinating inch of you."

Color filled her cheeks. "Zach, the others are listening—"

"I don't care." He laid a finger on her lips.

"I know you mentioned…love." Her voice hitched. "But we were trapped in the cave, thinking we might not make it out—"

He cupped her cheeks, tilting her head back to force her to meet his gaze. "So now you think I'll change my mind?"

"No one's ever wanted me like you do," she said, her tone charged with emotion.

He nuzzled her lips. "I want you more every day."

"God, I think I'm falling in love with you, too, Zach."

"Don't worry, you aren't alone. I'll be with you every step of the way." He grinned. "Now, let's get out of here. As soon as we can arrange it, I want you naked under me."

"Deal."

He yanked her close and kissed her. Around them, he heard her workmates whistling and catcalling.

"Knew you'd be next to take the fall, Kincaid," Hale called out.

"Better watch out," Declan warned. "You might be next, Hale."

The man looked aghast. "Nope. Not me." He jerked a thumb at Ronin. "Coop can go next."

The silent Ronin just raised a brow, and Zach had trouble imagining a woman brave enough to take on the dangerous-looking man.

It was a short trip back to the Treasure Hunter Security chopper. Callum climbed into the pilot's seat, Declan beside him. Soon, Zach found himself sitting in the back of the chopper, with Morgan leaning against his shoulder. As they took off, he stared out over the tsingy stone forest.

As interesting as it was, he was happy to be leaving.

As the THS team joked and talked around him, Zach stroked the amulet in his lap. He thought of Phaulkon and marveled at the artifact's journey. There was so much to learn from it, and the temple they'd left behind. A mystery to piece together and bring to light.

As the helicopter neared Tolagnaro airport, Zach felt odd, but relieved. They'd left here under dire circumstances...it was strange to be back and all in one piece.

Once the skids touched down, Declan opened the side door. "I radioed your team to let them know you were okay. They'll be happy to have you back."

"Thanks," Zach said.

"Except you're missing one student."

Zach tensed. "The Silk Road informant."

Declan nodded. "Max."

"Max?" Zach stared at the man incredulously.

"Yes. Charity's money came from a wealthy grandfather. Max's came from Silk Road."

"He didn't seem capable of hurting anybody."

"He didn't want to, and he broke down when we confronted him. His mother has a large gambling debt. Silk Road approached him, and offered him money to slip information to them. They provided him with a satellite phone."

"And let me guess," Morgan said, "after information, they kept wanting more and more."

Declan nodded. "They threatened his mother if he didn't attack you, Zach. He's drowning in remorse, but we've sent him back to the States for the authorities to deal with."

Shit, Max. Zach rubbed his temple. "Thanks, Declan."

He climbed out, and Morgan leaped out beside him.

"We have SUVs waiting," Declan said. "I guessed that you guys might like a night in Tolagnaro to rest. Darcy booked us rooms at one of the hotels. We'll rest up, and then head back to the *Storm Nymph* tomorrow."

"Sounds great." A big bed in a hotel sounded perfect. He had a few X-rated plans for the evening...after a long, hot shower and a nap. "Thanks for everything, Declan."

"Sure thing."

They'd taken a few steps away from the chopper, when they were suddenly surrounded by a black-clad team of soldiers aiming weapons at them.

Zach froze. The soldiers were all wearing black masks, which entirely hid their faces. Beside him, Morgan lifted her weapon in a lightning-fast move. Declan and the others did the same.

Nobody moved.

Chapter Nineteen

"Looks like we've got ourselves a standoff, here," Dec said.

Morgan kept her gun aimed at the soldier closest to her.

One of the soldiers stepped forward. "We don't want any trouble."

From one look at them, Morgan could tell they were experienced. These weren't mercenaries for hire. They held themselves ready, and their weapons weren't like anything Morgan had seen before. There was nothing about their black tactical gear that gave away who they were.

She caught Dec's eye, and he gave a tiny shake of his head. Dammit, it looked like Silk Road had wised up and hired the best.

Morgan's muscles bunched and she assessed her options. She could take down the one in front of her, then go left—

Suddenly, a soldier came out of nowhere and pressed his gun barrel to her neck.

"Don't even think about it." A menacing, deep voice.

"Delta, back off," the original man who'd spoken said.

After a humming second, the man pulled his weapon away from Morgan.

"We don't want to hurt anyone," the lead man said. "We just want the amulet."

"Silk Road is not getting the amulet," Morgan snapped.

The man stiffened. "We are not Silk Road."

"We're the opposite of Silk Road," another soldier to the leader's right, said. This one was female.

"The amulet is too dangerous," the leader continued. "We are here to safeguard it."

Morgan blinked and looked at Zach. He was watching the man carefully.

Zach cleared his throat. "The amulet is an artifact that deserves—"

The leader shook his head. "It needs to be somewhere where no one can misuse it."

"You can't believe it really has powers," Zach said.

But Morgan was thinking of how the giant lemurs had reacted. She glanced at the amulet, uncertain.

"We've been tasked with putting the amulet where Silk Road, and others like them, can never get their hands on it." The leader held out a gloved hand. "Please hand it over, Dr. James."

Relaxed and easy, Zach stepped forward and handed the amulet to the man.

Morgan took a step. "Zach—"

He shook his head. "The amulet isn't worth the loss of any more lives, or more people being hurt.

Besides, I think this guy might have a point."

The leader took it, slipping the amulet into a pocket on his combat trousers. As he did, Morgan saw his shirt shift at his wrist and caught a flash of silver. She frowned. It looked like his *skin* was silver.

She scanned the team of soldiers. Who the hell were these people?

"Thank you." The man lifted a hand, and suddenly his team started walking backward. They moved in tight formation, turned around the terminal building, and were gone.

Morgan looked at Dec and the others.

"What the fuck?" Cal said.

Instantly, her team rushed forward, weapons up. They circled the terminal building and saw...

Nothing. There was no sign of the man and his team in black.

"Fuck." Dec looked pissed.

"Who the hell were those guys?" Cal said.

"I don't know, but I plan to find out," Dec said darkly.

Morgan moved back to Zach. "Are you okay? I'm sorry we lost the amulet."

He shrugged. "All along, I was more interested in finding the *Soleil d'Orient*, really, and we still have that and all her other artifacts. The amulet was fascinating, but maybe it's better off this way." He looked into the distance. "Maybe the amulet was too dangerous."

She smiled. "You buying into the mystical resonance-technology theory?"

"Right now, I don't care." He wrapped an arm around her. "How does a night in a big bed sound? Followed by some wreck diving, and hot sex in a narrow ship bunk for the next few weeks?"

She leaned into him. "It sounds pretty darn good."

***

Hale leaned over the conference table at the Treasure Hunter Security warehouse, fiddling with a prototype grappling gun he was working on. He'd pulled it all apart, finetuned some parts, and was now trying to put it back together.

He heard the click of heels on the floor and looked up.

He let out a whistle. Morgan stopped to strike a pose. She was wearing a sleek, black dress, with a black coat over it. The outfit showed off her grade-A legs.

"Welcome back," he told her. "Nice tan."

Hale had returned to Denver from Madagascar a few weeks back, while Morgan had stayed on with Zach and his team to complete the diving on the *Soleil d'Orient*.

"What's with the dress?" He knew Morgan didn't like dressing up.

"I have a date," she told him, a smile crossing her face. "A third date."

It didn't take much to see that she was happy. Hale had known Morgan a while, and considered her a friend. She'd always had this edge...a sense of dissatisfaction. Like she was searching for something.

It seemed like she'd finally found that something, and it was Dr. Zachariah James.

"Zach been treating you right?" Hale asked.

Her smile widened. "Oh, yeah."

"No details, please." Hale shook his head and picked up one of his parts again. He'd been watching all his friends fall in love, lately. It was great to see them all happy, but it wasn't for him. He didn't want just one woman. There were so many lovely ladies out there, and so much variety to choose from. How could a guy possibly pick one?

For a second, black memories flashed in his head, before he clamped down on them. Besides, if you got close to one woman, it meant you had to share. He had things inside him that no woman should ever see.

"Any luck identifying the team in black?" she asked.

Hale shook his head. "It's driving Declan insane."

More heels clicked on the concrete floor. Darcy and Declan appeared.

"Hi, Morgan. Welcome home." Darcy gave Morgan a quick hug. "You look stunning, by the way. Zach won't know what hit him." Then Darcy's nose wrinkled. "Our mystery team is still just that, a mystery. There is no record of a team like that entering Madagascar. I've tapped my contacts and no one knows anything." She heaved out a frustrated sigh. "I even resorted to asking the FBI."

She said the acronym like it was poison.

Dec rolled his eyes. "She means Burke."

"Yeah," Morgan said. "I've noticed she doesn't like saying his name."

Darcy crossed her arms over her jewel-blue sweater. "The arrogant man just clammed up and gave me nothing. So much for sharing."

"It was for your own protection."

Everyone's heads whipped around. Hale saw that the man in question stood in the doorway, and he wasn't alone.

Hale studied the female agent with Burke. She was short, with long, blonde hair. Her features were attractive, but without a smile, they held an edge. She wore a dark suit, and Hale had to admit it showcased some nice, compact curves. As the agents approached, the woman's ponytail swung like a pendulum behind her.

"Burke." Dec came forward, holding out his hand. The two men shook.

"Nice to see you, Declan. Heard you had an interesting expedition in Madagascar." The agent's gaze moved to Darcy, and the two of them glared at each other.

Finally, Burke gestured to the woman with him. "This is Special Agent Elin Alexander. She is assisting me on the Silk Road investigation."

"Nice to meet you," the woman said in a neutral tone.

Hale had always had a thing for blondes, and this one intrigued him. She was so...cool and composed. There was no expression on her face, but he saw a sharp intelligence in her eyes.

"We'd like to know more about this mysterious team in black," Declan said. "I don't like anyone interfering on our jobs."

"It's best you forget you saw them," Burke answered. "All I can tell you is that they are the good guys, but they're dangerous. Just hope that you never see them again."

Declan sighed, rubbing the back of his neck. "That's it?"

"That's it."

"Fine. Why are you here?"

"I have a job for you," the agent said.

Hale set down his tools and leaned forward, his curiosity piqued.

Burke's intense gaze swept over them. "We've gotten intel on an expedition that Silk Road is planning. I want you to help me take them down."

Declan's gaze turned considering. Hale knew his boss was eager to see the end of Silk Road, once and for all.

"Go on," Dec said.

"Agent Alexander will be going undercover on the Silk Road team."

Hale's eyebrows shot up. Undercover?

"I've been working on infiltrating a local Silk Road group here in the US," the woman told them. "They are not the most...trusting people, but I've gotten to the point where I've been assigned to this expedition."

"Where's the expedition to?" Hale asked.

Pretty blue eyes met his. "Africa."

"You think this'll bring us one step closer to bringing the entire organization down?" Dec asked.

"I do," Agent Alexander said.

Even if it meant Agent Alexander had to walk into a nest of murderous thieves.

"We'd want your team to keep track of the expedition," Agent Burke said.

"Well, count me out of this one," Morgan said. "I have a date, and I'm still recovering from giant lemurs."

Burke frowned at her, before continuing. "I'd also like one of your men to get hired onto the expedition—"

Hale stood. "Count me in."

Dec shot him a sharp look, and Hale returned it steadily. He was the newest member of THS, but he knew he'd proved himself.

Finally, Dec nodded. "Hale's our man. All right, Burke, you have a deal."

***

"Here we go. One Sex on the Beach." Zach handed the cocktail to Morgan.

"I believe we've already done that." She winked at him as she sipped the orange-red drink, and leaned against the railing.

She made a sexy humming noise that arrowed straight to Zach's cock. It didn't matter how many times he'd had her, or how long he'd spent exploring her body, he still wanted her, more than ever.

They were on the rooftop deck of the museum. The sun was setting, and despite the cool, late-winter weather, she looked killer in her dress, shoulders covered by an aqua-blue wrap. Zach had pulled a few strings, and they had the entire place to themselves.

He leaned beside her. "Missing the Madagascan weather?"

She shook her head. "Maybe a tiny bit. But frankly, it's nice to be back."

"Come on, let's have dinner." He turned and pulled out a chair for her at the table he'd had set up. In the center was a fondue set, with melted chocolate and various pieces of cut-up fruit.

"You know me pretty well," she said.

He did. Every inch of her. Over the last few weeks, he'd spent his days diving the *Soleil d'Orient* and bringing up artifacts, and the nights exploring everything Morgan offered to him. They'd completed the dive, delivered the bulk of the artifacts to the Madagascan government, and brought back a collection of artifacts to Denver. He had a lot of research to conduct, and an exhibition to plan.

But this whole expedition had taught him that there were things in life that were more important than his work.

He sat, pulling his chair closer to hers. "I've got something to ask you." He pulled a small box from his pocket and set it on the table.

Her eyes went wide and her face turned an interesting shade of gray. She stared at the box like it was a hissing snake. "Zach...? Are you...?"

"What?" He suddenly realized what it looked like. "No! Not yet." He looked at her, a small smile flirting on his lips. "Why is your voice so high-pitched? You look terrified."

"So do you," she countered.

He shook his head. "I'm asking you to move in with me." He flicked open the small box. His front door key was nestled inside it. "I love you, Morgan. And one day, I'd like to talk about the M-word. But since getting you to agree to a third date took us being kidnapped, attacked by giant lemurs, and almost drowning, I thought I'd start with something a little simpler, first."

She was smiling, her eyes looking a little watery.

He smiled at her. "You tearing up?"

"No. I don't cry."

Sure. His tough Morgan with her prickly exterior and soft heart. "I want the adventure of you in my life. I love you, and while I came from nothing, I'm offering you love, laughter, adventure, and lots of hot sex."

"I love you, too, Zachariah James. I love the man you've made of yourself, and I'll take that love, laughter, adventure, and hot sex." She took the key, slipping it into the neckline of her dress. Then she cocked her head, her gaze warming. "So...how about we get started on the hot sex bit? I've always wanted to do it in a museum."

Instantly, Zach was hard as a rock. She pushed her chair back and stood, and he let her pull him to his feet, conscious she couldn't miss the raging hard-on tenting his trousers. He pulled her closer, sliding a hand under that maddening dress.

He moved his fingers up, then paused, desire throbbing through him.

"That's right," she murmured. "No underwear."

She started dragging him inside and shot him a sexy smile.

He found his voice. "There are cameras—"

"Lucky for you, your girlfriend is rather handy with security systems. Come on, Dr. James, time for us to have a new adventure."

I hope you enjoyed Morgan and Zach's story!

There are more Treasure Hunter Security adventures on the way! The series will continue with UNTRAVELED, Hale's story, out in mid-2017.

For more action-packed romance, read on for a preview of the first chapter of *Among Galactic Ruins,* the first book in my award-winning Phoenix Adventures series. This is action, adventure, romance and treasure hunting in space!

Preview: Among Galactic Ruins

MORE ACTION ROMANCE?

ACTION
ADVENTURE
TREASURE HUNTS
SEXY SCI-FI ROMANCE

As the descending starship hit turbulence, Dr. Alexa Carter gasped, her stomach jumping.

But she didn't feel sick, she felt *exhilarated.*

She stared out the window at the sand dunes of the planet below. Zerzura. The legendary planet packed with danger, mystery and history.

She was *finally* here. All she could see was sand dune, after yellow sand dune, all the way off into the distance. The dual suns hung in the sky, big and full—one gold and one red—baking the ground below.

But there was more to Zerzura than that. She knew, from all her extensive history training as an astro-archeologist, that the planet was covered in ruins—some old and others beyond ancient. She knew every single one of the myths and legends.

She glanced down at her lap and clutched the

Sync communicator she was holding. Right here she had her ticket to finding an ancient Terran treasure.

Lexa thumbed the screen. She'd found the slim, ancient vase in the museum archives and initially thought nothing of the lovely etchings of priestesses on the side of it.

Until she'd finished translating the obscure text.

She'd been gobsmacked when she realized the text gave her clues that not only formed a map, but also described what the treasure was at the end. A famed Fabergé egg.

Excitement zapped like electricity through her veins. After a career spent mostly in the Galactic Institute of Historical Preservation and on a few boring digs in the central systems, she was now the curator of the Darend Museum on Zeta Volantis—a private and well-funded museum that was mostly just a place for her wealthy patron, Marius Darend, to house his extensive, private collection of invaluable artifacts from around the galaxy.

But like most in the galaxy, he had a special obsession with old Earth artifacts. When she'd gone to him with the map and proposal to go on a treasure hunt to Zerzura to recover it, he'd been more than happy to fund it.

So here she was, Dr. Alexa Carter, on a treasure hunt.

Her father, of course, had almost had a coronary when she'd told her parents she'd be gone for several weeks. That familiar hard feeling invaded her belly. Baron Carter did not like his only daughter working, let alone being an astro-archeologist, and he *really* didn't like her going to a planet like Zerzura. He'd ranted about wild chases and wastes of time, and predicted her failure.

She straightened in her seat. She'd been ignoring her father's disapproval for years. When she had the egg in her hands, then he'd have to swallow his words.

Someone leaned over her, a broad shoulder brushing hers. "Strap in, Princess, we're about to land."

Lexa's excitement deflated a little. There was just one fly in her med gel.

Unfortunately, Marius had insisted she bring along the museum's new head of security. She didn't know much about Damon Malik, but she knew she didn't like him. The rumor among the museum staff was that he had a super-secret military background.

She looked at him now, all long, and lean and dark. He had hair as black as her own, but skin far darker. She couldn't see him in the military. His manner was too...well, she wasn't sure what, exactly, but he certainly didn't seem the type to happily take orders.

No, he preferred to be the one giving them.

He shot her a small smile, but it didn't reach his dark eyes. Those midnight-blue eyes were always...intense. Piercing. Like he was assessing everything, calculating. She found it unsettling.

"I'm already strapped in, Mr. Malik." She tugged on her harness and raised a brow.

"Just checking. I'm here to make sure you don't get hurt on this little escapade."

"Escapade?" She bit her tongue and counted to ten. "We have a map leading to the location of a very valuable artifact. That's hardly an escapade."

"Whatever helps you sleep at night, Princess." He shot a glance at the window and the unforgiving desert below. "This is a foolish risk for some silly egg."

She huffed out a breath. Infuriating man. "Why get a job at a museum if you think artifacts are silly?"

He leaned back in his seat. "Because I needed a change. One where no one tried to kill me."

Kill him? She narrowed her eyes and wondered again just what the hell he'd done before he'd arrived at the Darend.

A chime sounded and the pilot's voice filtered into the plush cabin of Marius' starship. "Landing at Kharga spaceport in three minutes. Hang on, ladies and gentlemen."

Excitement filled Lexa's belly. Ignoring the man beside her, she looked out the window again.

The town of Kharga was visible now. They flew directly over it, and she marveled at the primitive look and the rough architecture. The buildings were made of stone—some simple squares, others with domed roofs, and some a haphazard sprawl of both. In the dirt-lined streets, ragged beasts were led by robed locals, and battered desert speeders flew in every direction, hovering off the ground.

It wasn't advanced and yes, it was rough and

dangerous. So very different to the marble-lined floors and grandeur of the Darend Museum or the Institute's huge, imposing museums and research centers. And it was the complete opposite of the luxury she'd grown up with in the central systems.

She barely resisted bouncing in her seat like a child. She couldn't *wait* to get down there. She wasn't stupid, she knew there were risks, but could hold her own and she knew when to ask for help.

The ship touched down, a cloud of dust puffing past the window. Lexa ripped her harness off, trying—and failing—to contain her excitement.

"Wait." Damon grabbed her arm and pulled her back from the opening door. "I'll go first."

As he moved forward, she pulled a face at his broad back. *Arrogant know-it-all.*

The door opened with a quiet hiss. She watched him stop at the top of the three steps that had extended from the starship. He scanned the spaceport...well, spaceport was a generous word for it. Lexa wasn't sure the sandy ground, beaten-up starships lined up beside them, and the battered buildings covered with black streaks—were those laser scorch marks?—warranted the term spaceport, but it was what it was.

Damon checked the laser pistols holstered at his lean hips then nodded. "All right." He headed down the steps.

Lexa tugged on the white shirt tucked into her fitted khaki pants. Mr. Dark and Brooding might be dressed in all black, but she'd finally pulled her rarely used expedition clothes out of her closet for the trip. She couldn't wait to get them dirty. She tucked her Sync into her small backpack, swung the bag over her shoulder and headed down the stairs.

"Our contact is supposed to meet us here." She looked around but didn't see anyone paying them much attention. A rough-looking freighter crew lounged near a starfreighter that didn't even look like it could make it off the ground. A couple of robed humanoids argued with three smaller-statured reptilians. "He's a local treasure hunter called Brocken Phoenix."

Damon grunted. "Looks like he's late. I suggest we head to the central market and ask around."

"Okay." She was eager to see more of Kharga and soak it all in.

"Stay close to me."

Did he have to use that autocratic tone all the time? She tossed him a salute.

Something moved through his dark eyes before he shook his head and started off down the dusty street.

As they neared the market, the crowds thickened. The noise increased as well. People had set up makeshift stalls, tables, and tents and were selling...well, just about everything.

There was a hawker calling out the features of his droids. Lexa raised a brow. The array available was interesting—from stocky maintenance droids to life-like syndroids made to look like humans. Other sellers were offering clothes, food, weapons, collectibles, even dragon bones.

Then she saw the cages.

She gasped. "Slavers."

Damon looked over and his face hardened. "Yeah."

The first cage held men. All tall and well-built. Laborers. The second held women. Anger shot through her. "It can't be legal."

"We're a long way from the central systems, Princess. You'll find lots of stuff here on Zerzura that isn't legal."

"We have to—"

He raised a lazy brow. "Do something? Unless you've got a whole bunch of e-creds I don't know about or an army in your back pocket, there isn't much we can do."

Her stomach turned over and she looked away. He might be right, but did he have to be so cold about it?

"Look." He pointed deeper into the market at a dusty, domed building with a glowing neon sign above the door. "That bar is where I hear the treasure hunters gather."

She wondered how he'd heard anything about the place when they'd only been dirtside a few minutes. But she followed him toward the bar, casting one last glance at the slaves.

As they neared the building, a body flew outward through the arched doorway. The man hit the dirt, groaning. He tried to stand before flopping face first back into the sand.

Even from where they stood, Lexa smelled the liquor fumes wafting off him. Nothing smooth and sweet like what was available back on Zeta Volantis. No, this smelled like homebrewed rotgut.

Damon stepped over the man with barely a glance. At the bar entrance, he paused. "I think you should stay out here. It'll be safer. I'll find out what I can about Phoenix and be right back."

She wanted to argue, but right then, two huge giants slammed out of the bar, wrestling each other. One was an enormous man, almost seven feet tall, with some aquatic heritage. He had pale-blue skin, large, wide-set eyes and tiny gills on the side of his neck. His opponent was human with a mass of dreadlocked brown hair, who stood almost as tall and broad.

The human slammed a giant fist into the aquatic's face, shouting in a language Lexa's lingual implant didn't recognize. That's when Lexa realized the dreadlocked man was actually a woman.

A security droid floated out of the bar. Its laser weapons swiveled to aim at the fighting pair. "You are no longer welcome at the Desert Dragon. Please vacate the premises."

Grumbling, the fighters pulled apart, then shuffled off down the street.

Lexa swallowed. "Fine. I'll stay out here."

"Stay close," Damon warned.

She tossed him another mock salute and when he scowled, she felt a savage sense of satisfaction. Then he turned and ducked inside.

She turned back to study the street. One building down, she saw a stall holder standing behind a table covered in what looked like small artifacts. Lexa's heart thumped. She had to take a look.

"All original. Found here on Zerzura." The older man spread his arms out over his wares. "Very, very old." His eyes glowed in his ageless face topped by salt-and-pepper hair. "Very valuable."

"May I?" Lexa indicated a small, weathered statue.

The man nodded. "But you break, you buy."

Lexa studied the small figurine. It was supposed to resemble a Terran fertility statue—a woman with generous hips and breasts. She tested the weight of it before she sniffed and set it down. "It's not a very good fake. I'd say you create a wire mesh frame, set it in a mold, then pour a synthetic plas in. You finish it off by spraying it with some sort of rock texture."

The man's mouth slid into a frown.

Lexa studied the other items. Jewelry, small boxes and inscribed stones. She fingered a necklace. It was by no means old but it was pretty.

Then she spotted it.

A small, red egg, covered in gold-metalwork and resting on a little stand.

She picked it up, cradling its slight weight. The craftwork was terrible but there was no doubt it was a replica of a Fabergé egg.

"What is this?" she asked the man.

He shrugged. "Lots of myths about the Orphic Priestesses around here. They lived over a thousand years ago and the egg was their symbol."

Lexa stroked the egg.

The man's keen eyes narrowed in on her. "It's a pretty piece. Said to be made in the image of the priestesses' most valuable treasure, the Goddess Egg. It was covered in Terran rubies and gold."

A basic history. Lexa knew from her research that the Goddess Egg had been brought to Zerzura by Terran colonists escaping the Terran war and had been made by a famed jeweler on Earth named Fabergé. Unfortunately, most of its history had been lost.

Someone bumped into Lexa from behind. She ignored it, shifting closer to the table.

Then a hard hand clamped down on her elbow and jerked her backward. The little red egg fell into the sand.

Lexa expected the cranky stall owner to squawk about the egg and demand payment. Instead, he scampered backward with wide eyes and turned away.

Lexa's accoster jerked her around.

"Hey," she exclaimed.

Then she looked up. Way up.

The man was part-reptilian, with iridescent scales covering his enormous frame. He stood somewhere over six and a half feet with a tough face that looked squashed.

"Let me go." She slapped at his hand. *Idiot.*

He was startled for a second and did release her. Then he scowled, which turned his face from frightening to terrifying. "Give me your e-creds." He grabbed her arm, large fingers biting into her flesh, and shook her. "I want everything transferred to my account."

Lexa raised a brow. "Or what?"

With his other hand, he withdrew a knife the length of her forearm. "Or I use this."

Also by Anna Hackett

Treasure Hunter Security
Undiscovered
Uncharted
Unexplored
Unfathomed

Galactic Gladiators
Gladiator
Warrior
Hero
Protector

Hell Squad
Marcus
Cruz
Gabe
Reed
Roth
Noah
Shaw
Holmes
Niko
Finn
Devlin

The Anomaly Series
Time Thief
Mind Raider
Soul Stealer
Salvation
Anomaly Series Box Set

The Phoenix Adventures
Among Galactic Ruins
At Star's End
In the Devil's Nebula
On a Rogue Planet
Beneath a Trojan Moon
Beyond Galaxy's Edge
On a Cyborg Planet
Return to Dark Earth
On a Barbarian World
Lost in Barbarian Space
Through Uncharted Space

Perma Series
Winter Fusion

The WindKeepers Series
Wind Kissed, Fire Bound
Taken by the South Wind
Tempting the West Wind
Defying the North Wind
Claiming the East Wind

Standalone Titles
Savage Dragon
Hunter's Surrender
One Night with the Wolf

Anthologies
A Galactic Holiday
Moonlight (UK only)
Vampire Hunter (UK only)
Awakening the Dragon (UK Only)

For more information visit AnnaHackettBooks.com

About the Author

I'm a USA Today bestselling author and I'm passionate about ***action romance***. I love stories that combine the thrill of falling in love with the excitement of action, danger and adventure. I'm a sucker for that moment when the team is walking in slow motion, shoulder-to-shoulder heading off into battle.

I write about people overcoming unbeatable odds and achieving seemingly impossible goals. I like to believe it's possible for all of us to do the same.

My books are mixture of action, adventure and sexy romance and they're recommended for anyone who enjoys fast-paced stories where the boy wins the girl at the end (or sometimes the girl wins the boy!)

For release dates, action romance info, free books, and other fun stuff, sign up for the latest news here:

Website: AnnaHackettBooks.com

CPSIA information can be obtained
at www.ICGtesting.com
Printed in the USA
LVHW03s1708180818
587386LV00001B/46/P